מסורה

ArtScroll Youth Series®

The Best of
Olomeinu

BOOK THREE

The Best of

Compiled from the pages of
Olomeinu
by
Rabbi Yaakov Fruchter

Edited for publication by
Rabbi Nosson Scherman

Illustrated by
Yosef Dershowitz
Designed by
Sheah Brander

BOOK THREE

OUR WORLD עולמנו

Olomeinu®

CHANUKAH AND OTHER STORIES

*An anthology of 20 exciting, inspiring and
beautifully illustrated stories for young and old.*

Published by

Mesorah Publications, ltd

in conjunction with
Torah Umesorah
National Society for Hebrew Day Schools

FIRST EDITION
First Impression ... October, 1982

Published and Distributed by
MESORAH PUBLICATIONS, Ltd.
1969 Coney Island Avenue
Brooklyn, New York 11223

Also available to schools and students through
TORAH UMESORAH PUBLICATIONS
229 Park Avenue South
New York, N.Y. 10003

Distributed in Israel by
MESORAH MAFITZIM / J. GROSSMAN
Rechov Bayit Vegan 90/5
Jerusalem, Israel

Distributed in Europe by
J. LEHMANN HEBREW BOOKSELLERS
20 Cambridge Terrace
Gateshead, Tyne and Wear
England NE8 1RP

ARTSCROLL YOUTH SERIES®
THE BEST OF OLOMEINU / Book III: Chanukah and Other Stories
© *Copyright 1982 by* MESORAH PUBLICATIONS,Ltd.

The stories in this volume have appeared in the pages of
OLOMEINU — OUR WORLD
published by
TORAH UMESORAH / National Society for Hebrew Day Schools
229 Park Avenue South, New York, N.Y. 10003
Copyright and all rights reserved by Torah Umesorah.

ALL RIGHTS RESERVED.

*These stories, new illustrations, and associated textual contents
— including the typographic layout, cover artwork, and ornamental graphics—
have been designed, edited and revised as to content form and style.*

No part of this book may be reproduced, stored, or copied **in any form**
without **written** *permission from the copyright holders,
except by a reviewer who wishes to quote brief passages in connection with a review
written for inclusion in magazines or newspapers.*

THE RIGHTS OF THE COPYRIGHT HOLDERS WILL BE STRICTLY ENFORCED.

ISBN
0-89906-754-9 (hard cover)
0-89906-755-7 (paperback)

Typography by CompuScribe at ArtScroll Studios, Ltd.
1969 Coney Island Avenue / Brooklyn, N.Y. 11223 / (212) 339-1700

בס''ד

A*s a Chanukah gift to Jewish children*

throughout the world,

Mr. and Mrs. Sidney Hoffman and Family

Bridgeport, Connecticut

are dedicating this edition of

The Best of Olomeinu/

Chanukah and Other Stories

in honor of the devoted lay leaders,

administrators, faculty members and students

of the Torah Umesorah Hebrew Day Schools

who are, indeed, the future hope of Israel.

Tishrei 5743
October 1982

Preface

בס"ד

As we present the public with Book Three in the series of *The Best of Olomeinu* story anthologies, we again offer a *Shevach V'hodoyah* to *Hashem Yisborach* for enabling us to continue providing young people with wholesome reading material culled from the "treasures" of Torah Umesorah's popular children's magazine OLOMEINU/OUR WORLD.

Less than a year has passed since this series was born. In this brief time, the enthusiastic response of young and old to the previous volumes has given us the impetus to publish this third one — the *Chut Hameshulash* — of an increasingly popular series.

Most of the stories in this volume deal with Chanukah. These stories span many centuries: the period of the Crusades, the time of the Spanish Inquisition, the Holocaust in Europe, and the heroic struggle of Jews in modern day Russia.

The theme of Chanukah — namely Israel's unswerving and uncompromising dedication and rededication to Torah and *mitzvos* through מְסִירַת נֶפֶשׁ (self sacrifice) and אֱמוּנָה פְּשׁוּטָה (simple faith) — permeates these stories. And as stated in the prefaces to Volumes One and Two, OLOMEINU and this series of anthologies share a primary purpose: to preserve, strengthen —

and rekindle if necessary — the אֱמוּנָה פְּשׁוּטָה inherent in the *neshamah* of every Jewish child. We pray, therefore, that the selection of stories in this volume will go a long way in helping us attain our goal.

We take this opportunity to thank the writers of the stories and all those whose tireless and devoted efforts have helped make this volume a reality בעזהש"י.

אסרו חג סוכות תשמ"ג

Rabbi Yaakov Fruchter
Managing Editor, Olomeinu/Our World
Director, Torah Umesorah Publications

Table of Contents

The Mysterious Chanukah Menorah

by Dr. Gershon Kranzler

The synagogue in Eisenstadt, Germany, was one of the oldest in Europe. In 1937, the Germans destroyed it. In the middle 1800's, however, it was the pride of the thriving Jewish community that lived near it. Many came to see and admire the simple, sturdy, holy building that had stood for many centuries, one stone firmly on the other.

In 1847, a young boy from a small village came to stay with his uncle in Eisenstadt for the *Chanukah* holiday. The first night of *Chanukah,* he and his uncle went to the *shul* for evening prayers, at which time the Rabbi lit the single candle in the large, gold *menorah.* After the *davening* all the people went to their homes to light their own candles and to celebrate *Chanukah* in a friendly spirit. But the young visitor asked his uncle for permission to stay behind. He had never been inside this *shul* before, and he wanted to look over the old building. And so, when his uncle left, he began to walk around and look at the ceiling and the walls … Then he noticed the *shammos* (caretaker) up front.

The *shammos,* thinking he was alone, went up to the Holy Ark, opened it, and seemed to be puttering with something inside. The boy went up to see what he was doing. Strangely, the

shammos had put a candle into a small silver *menorah* standing in the left hand corner of the Ark, and now he was lighting it. The boy's curiosity was too strong. He made a noise, and as the *shammos* turned around, he walked up to him. "Forgive me, sir, I couldn't help seeing what you did. Please tell me, why is that small *menorah* in the Ark and why did you light it?"

"Well," said the *shammos*, "it's a story passed on from one *shammos* to the other. Nobody else here knows about it, but there's no harm in telling you. Sit down, my son, and I'll tell you."

It was in the 1200's. The Second Crusade was under way. Thousands of peasants became soldiers overnight and marched across Europe to fight the Moslems who had conquered the Holy Land. It was an adventure for them, and their religious leaders promised to reward them. So the ignorant peasants banded together and marched. And the first thing they did was massacre the Jews wherever they went.

At first it seemed the Jews of Eisenstadt were going to escape. The mob of peasants was a good fifty miles away. But then the dread news hit the town. The mob had decided to turn off and take care of the Eisenstadt Jews before going further. The Jews, terrified, ran to their rabbi and asked what to do.

Calmly, Rabbi Asher replied, "It is late in the afternoon. Let us assemble in the *shul* for afternoon and evening prayers. And do not put terror in the hearts of others. As *Hashem* wishes, so shall be our fate."

Swiftly the men, women and children came to the *shul*. The *davening* that afternoon was unlike any other. Every word was said slowly, clearly, its meaning fully understood, and tears came often from the worshipers who were facing massacre and sure death. The children looked at their parents. They did not know what had happened, but the fright and terror spread to their hearts, and they were afraid. The *shammos* bolted and barricaded the heavy doors. There was no need to leave the doors open any more. Every Jew in Eisenstadt was inside that *shul.*

Then they began saying *Tehillim* (Psalms). Sentence by sentence they recited the pleas for help from the Book of Psalms. Those who were near the windows occasionally heard a rumble from far away, and they turned to their Psalms even more fervently. Outside the *shul,* the low rumbles came nearer and nearer. Soon everyone could hear them clearly. The mob was nearing, crying aloud for blood. The prayer reached a climax. A great wailing and sobbing filled that large room. Soon the mob would be here. The walls seemed to shake with the anguished prayers, and terror seized the people.

It was the first night of *Chanukah.* Whatever will happen, the first candle must be lit. The Rabbi motioned to the *shammos,* who nodded and brought the box of candles. Then the Rabbi walked toward the *menorah* that always stood on a shelf on the south wall. All eyes turned toward that wall, and then someone cried, "It's gone." The *menorah* was not there! But there was no time to think about that now. The bloodcurdling cries of the mob could be heard by the weeping, terrified Jews of Eisenstadt. Within a short time the mob would be here. Everyone gave way to despair. Men, women and children cried and wailed. The Rabbi went up before the Ark and asked for silence. All crying stopped at once. They looked up, wondering what the Rabbi would say in these last moments.

"Tonight," the Rabbi began, "is the beginning of *Chanukah*. At this time, many years ago, our forefathers were saved from being wiped out. Tonight we cannot celebrate this holiday, because our *menorah* is lost. But if we are worthy of it, another miracle of *Chanukah* can happen tonight. All is possible for *Hashem*. Even when the sword lies on his throat, the Jew does not give up hope. Are we not the servants, even the children of *Hashem?* Then do not give up all hope. Until the last moment let us pray; and if that moment should come, let us know and understand that so is the will of the Holy One, Blessed is He, and let us meet our death as loyal Jews."

Everyone remained silent. Only the sounds of the frenzied mob filled the air. Then the *shammos* suddenly exclaimed, "I remember!" Everyone looked at him, startled. He went on, "I remember now. There is another *menorah* in the Ark, down in the left hand corner. I knew I saw one, but I couldn't remember where I'd seen it." And the Rabbi said, "Praised is *Hashem,* for He has enabled us to keep this *mitzvah* of observing *Chanukah.*" He opened the Ark and reached down into the left hand corner. His hand grasped the *menorah* and pulled. The *menorah* wouldn't budge.

In the meantime, the mob, finding the homes of the Jews empty, turned toward the *shul,* more infuriated than ever at the trick these Jews had played on them. The Jews, they thought, had no right to stay away from their homes and fool these "upright, religious" soldiers. They, the mob, would teach those Jews what

it meant to fool "holy" crusaders.

The Rabbi pulled and pulled at the *menorah*. It stuck fast. He tried to turn it. And strangely, it turned freely. He turned and turned, and then he looked down calmly but closely. His eyes were fooling him. It couldn't be true. But yes, it was really happening before his eyes. The platform in front of the Ark, on which he was standing, was moving inward. Below was a stone staircase. Like an electric shock the news spread through the crowd. The Rabbi began directing everyone down the stairs, and as each one went down, he took with him one of the Torahs that stood in the Ark. They could not be left behind, for the mob would desecrate them.

As the men, women and children filed down the stone staircase, they could hear the mob pounding with fury against the heavy doors of the *shul*. The Rabbi then shut the doors of the Ark, went down the stairs, and pulled the platform board to its regular position. As he did so, he heard the *shul* doors crash and splinter. While the mob let their wrath out on the empty seats, the Jews walked along an underground tunnel to safety many miles away. The tunnel ended in a large underground chamber, with ladders all around leading to trap doors. Everyone waited for the Rabbi to join them. He came forward and stood before them. He spoke, "In peril we turned to our Creator; let us not forget Him now that the danger is past. Let us say *Hallel*" (Psalms of thanksgiving to *Hashem*). In that underground room cut out in the earth, they all recited *Hallel* with great fervor. When they had finished, the Rabbi went to one of the walls and made a little niche by removing some of the earth with his fingers. Just above this little shelf-in-the-wall he made another just like it. In each he stuck a candle, and then he lighted the top one. With this he lit the lower one, after chanting the blessings for *Chanukah* candles. While they burned brightly, lighting up the chamber, no one spoke. They all looked at the candles, and they seemed to understand exactly what the candles were trying to say. They understood the message of *Chanukah*, the promise of rescue to those who deserve it.

This was the story the *shammos* told the boy that night in the *shul*. Then the *shammos* spoke, "Many weeks later, the Jews were again fully settled in Eisenstadt and the *shul* was repaired. And from then on, every year on the first night of *Chanukah*, the *shammos* of the *shul* lights one candle in the small *menorah* down in the left hand corner of the Ark. Now go home to your uncle. He is surely wondering what is keeping you here."

Chanukah, 1492

by Rochel Feder

She sat by the fireplace in her bedroom, sewing. Such a beautiful room it was, with its soft velvet drapes, and huge crystal chandelier. But Donna Miriam found no pleasure in the beauty of her home, just as she failed to enjoy her expensive jewelry and silken robes. Gladly would she give away everything, every diamond necklace, every last one of her elegant gowns, if only … She sighed, a deep, heartrending sigh … It was useless to think of things that could never be …

And so she sewed a small bag of *Chanukah* candles into the lining of her husband's coat. "A Jew is a Jew no matter where he is," she thought. Her stitches were neat and careful at first. So much love, so much feeling were put into every single stitch. But after a while, they weren't so neat anymore, for her eyes were blurred with tears and she could not see …

Two nights later a loud knocking awakened the family from its sleep. It was useless to run; there was no place to run to.

The officer's eyes gleamed with hatred and cruelty as he faced her husband. "Don Manuel, you are under arrest. Get dressed immediately and come with us!"

Don Manuel was prepared. In a way he felt strangely relieved, now that the tension, the waiting, was finally over. "I would like a moment with my family," he quietly said.

The officer was enjoying himself. He seemed to relish seeing the anguish that was written all over Donna Miriam's white face, the pain and terror in her dark eyes. "All right!", he barked. "But only a moment!"

Don Manuel got dressed and gathered his dear ones to him. "Be brave, my children ... and you, Miriam, be brave and strong. Never forget what we are."

Donna Miriam could hardly speak. "The candles," she whispered, "the candles."

"Yes, Miriam, I have them. I'll use them."

"What's taking you so long?" roared the officer, grabbing Don Manuel by the collar and dragging him to the door. "Get going!" And out they went, into the night.

Marranos they were ... Secret Jews ... They did not ask for much, these Jews. What they wanted was to be able to sit unafraid at a truly Jewish *Shabbos* table and sing *zemiros* (*Shabbos* songs) in voices loud and clear ... to have a Jewish *seder* with wine and *matzos* and all the rest ... to hear the sweet voice of a child asking the "Four Questions" and not be afraid that soon may come a loud knocking on the door ... to hold an *esrog* on *Succos* ... and to live in a *succah*.

How these people wished for their children to have the pleasure and excitement of getting dressed up on *Purim,* to go out into the sunshine with plates of *shloach monos* (*Purim* gifts) for family and friends ... Their hearts cried out for the simple joy of putting on *tefillin,* the feel of the leather straps wound around the arm ...

Marranos ... Secret Jews ... This was their sin, their only crime, because these were the days of the Spanish Inquisition when it was a crime to be a Jew, a crime for which men were torn from their families and cruelly tortured until they died. As much as they tried to keep their "crimes" secret, there were always too many enemies, too many spies. Sometimes it was a "devoted" servant who suddenly realized that if she would tell about the two sets of dishes in the kosher kitchen, she would be richly rewarded and wouldn't have to work as a maid any more. Or maybe somebody noticed that a little boy was wearing those "Jewish strings," those *"tzitzis"* under his shirt. How careful they were that nobody should notice these things, but sometimes, too many times, they were noticed and then it was too late.

Too late, too late. That was why poor Donna Miriam was home alone now with her children, weeping into her pillow throughout the long nights — wondering if her turn would come and if she would hear the loud knocking again.

It is the first night of *Chanukah*. The cell is black, pitch dark … Suddenly, a little flame … one small, glowing little bit of fire … And then, a few moments later, another precious little bit of fire … *"Baruch atah Hashem … asher kideshanu b'mitzvotav … l'hadlik ner shel Chanukah … sheasah nissim la'avoteinu … bayamim haheim, bazman hazeh."* A man stands before the little flames, his whole body swaying, shaking, back and forth, back and forth, like a branch in the wind … *"Baruch atah Hashem … shehecheyanu v'keyemanu, v'hegeanu lazman hazeh."* You have performed miracles before, *Hashem*. Perhaps a miracle will happen now again. And even if I must die because I am a Jew, I thank You for allowing me to live for one last *Chanukah*. The little flames, the precious candles … they set his face aflame with a wonderful fire … as he sways back and forth, back and forth … and all the while tears fall from his eyes and roll down his face, into his graying beard.

Just imagine the feeling of this man on this first night of *Chanukah!* The first *Chanukah* away from his home, away from his family — in a black cell, a dungeon, where he has known only hunger and beatings and indescribable torture. And yet he remembers to take out his candles, those precious little candles that his good wife Donna Miriam remembered to prepare, and in the middle of cruel Spain, he celebrates *Chanukah*.

The guard outside Don Manuel's cell yawned sleepily. It was late and he was tired and eager to go home and get some sleep. "Oh well," he thought, "just one more hour and I'll be through for the day." Soon he dozed off and had a dream. He was a little boy again and his Jewish neighbors were celebrating one of their holidays. He could hear them singing and he could see them standing by their window, with the little lamp and the little flames …

His family and friends all hated Jews and would gladly see them dead, and he also hated them. It was a natural thing to do, to hate Jews, just as it was natural to eat and sleep and get drunk on Saturday nights. But these Jewish neighbors were different, somehow. He couldn't hate them, as much as he wanted to. He'd always been tall for his age, too tall, and chubby too, with a thick bunch of curly black hair and ugly freckles all over his face. The neighborhood kids were always making fun of him, calling him names and throwing stones at him, just as they did to the Jewish boys. They never called him by his real name. It was always "Curly" or "Fatty" or "Gorgeous." They never let him join in their games, but that he didn't mind much. He knew that if he played with them he'd only make a fool of himself, clumsy and awkward as he was. But those Jews, next door, they were always nice … They always called him Pedro and greeted him with a smile and a friendly "hello." When they made a special *Shabbos* or holiday dish, they always gave him some to nibble on. In his dream it was *Chanukah* and he was in the Jewish house happily eating a plate of crispy potato pancakes. Mmm … they were

good, those crispy, golden brown *latkes!* He could still smell them now, in his sleep. That smell always came together with the singing by the window and the little lamp with the lights.

He shook himself awake and looked around. About a half hour to go. He sat there a while, still groggy with sleep, thinking about his little dream. And then he heard it … that singing again … softly, very, very softly, only this time it was real and not a dream … It was coming from his prisoner's cell, only a few feet away. "Why, that dirty Jew!" he thought, wild with rage. "I'll teach him to sing his crazy songs here!"

He rushed for the door and threw it open, the urge to kill boiling within him. "What's going on here?" he roared, lunging forward, like an animal about to tear into its prey.

Suddenly he stopped, as if paralyzed, unable to move, his mouth open, yet unable to speak … little lights … small, flickering bits of flame … memories of childhood … the Jews next door … and that awful day, when a group of neighborhood toughs ganged up against him only because he was ugly and clumsy and they wanted a little fun. There were about twenty of them and they all came chasing after him, throwing pebbles. And he ran — like a frightened, wounded animal he ran, until, exhausted, he reached his house. Frantically, sobbing, he banged on the door, the gang of boys only a few feet away. The door did not open! His mother wasn't home!

But the Jewish lady next door, she suddenly appeared, out of nowhere. She rescued him and dragged him quickly into her home. She sat him down by the stove in her cozy kitchen that smelled so nice, and gave him a plateful of *latkes* to eat. The warmth in that kitchen and the kindness in the woman's voice, comforted him … And now, suddenly, he remembered it all, remembered it as if it had happened yesterday. He looked at Don Manuel, a battered, painfilled, hungry Jew who was hated and tormented by all of mighty Spain. Pedro turned from the Jew who stood by the little flames and slowly walked away … Gently, very gently, he closed the door behind him.

Shezazkile

by Rabbi Solomon Rosenbluth

High above, on the peaceful mountains of Judea surrounding Jerusalem, grew an olive tree. There was nothing unusual about this tree except that on this tree lived a little olive named Shezazkile. Shezazkile's one great ambition was that, when he would grow up, he would be made into oil for the golden *Menorah,* which burned brightly in the *Beis Hamikdash.*

Shezazkile's neighbors teased him. They would say, "How do you know if you will be fit for *Menorah* oil? Even if you grow up to be worthy to be used in the lamp, will the *Kohen* choose you from among the many other olives to use for the *Menorah?*"

The only thing Shezazkile could answer was — "I just know! I have a feeling!" The other olives would laugh and make fun of his answers.

As the time of the harvest came nearer and nearer, the little olive was careful to eat all his food and to listen to whatever advice he was given that would help him grow into a big olive. Then the harvest came. All the olives were plucked from the trees that fed them, and they were then thrown into dark, cold sacks. Shezazkile found himself among the many olives being brought into Jerusalem for sale in the city markets. The memory of his friends' voices teasing him about his one great ambition to become oil for the *Menorah* of the *Beis Hamikdash* kept going around in his mind. He felt cold and frightened in the gloomy sack, and wondered what would become of him now. Finally he found himself thrown onto a rickety wagon.

After a long and weary ride, the wagon stopped and suddenly the bright sun started pouring upon him as the sack in which he was lying was opened. Lo and behold, he was in the market place in Jerusalem.

People from all over the country came to bid for the olives. Some were bought by the city to be pressed into oil for the street lamps, others were bought by merchants who would sell the oil for *Shabbos* lights, and others went to the very wealthy to provide light for all the rooms of their homes. Our little olive wondered which class he would fall into. Suddenly, there was a hush in the market place. The figure of a tall, thin man with a beard as white as snow appeared. He was none other than the *Kohen Gadol* who had come to buy olives for use in the *Beis Hamikdash.* Shezazkile was once again picked up, brought to a factory where he was made into oil, and poured into a flask. How happy Shezazkile was when he saw that his dream had been realized. Shezazkile had been made into oil for the golden *Menorah* in the *Beis Hamikdash.* Then, he was given a special honor. On the flask in which Shezazkile was poured, the *Kohen Gadol* put his own seal — something that he hardly ever did!

Now Shezazkile found himself among many other flasks to be used for the *Menorah.* Day after day he waited for his turn to kindle the lamp. Finally his turn came. However, on that day the Syrians broke into the *Beis Hamikdash.* They destroyed

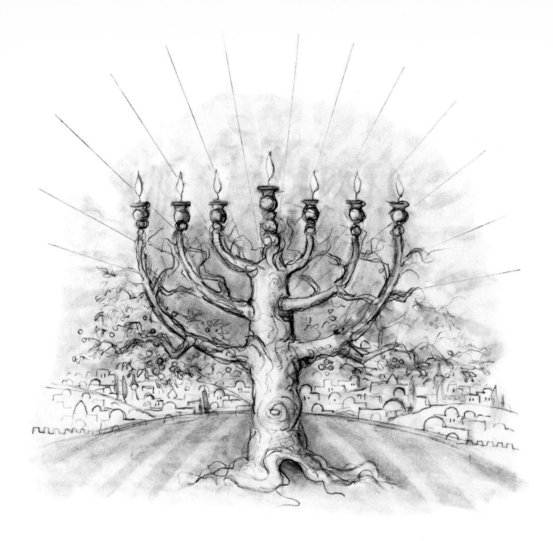

practically every holy thing in sight. They smashed every flask of holy oil. If not for the foresight of one of the priests, Shezazkile, too, would have been destroyed. Instead he was hidden in a dark, dingy corner.

How much woe there was in the heart of Shezazkile! All his life he had prayed that he be burned in the *Menorah* and finally when his turn had come, he had been placed instead into this miserable corner to be forgotten.

The Jews fought the Syrians with prayers in their hearts that *Hashem* would help them drive out the enemy from the *Beis Hamikdash* and they would once again cleanse it and serve *Hashem* there.

But this took several years. Shezazkile felt himself getting old. He wondered if he would ever be able to light any kind of lamp, let alone the golden *Menorah.* Finally, one day, he heard a great deal of shouting. The news reached him that Yehudah the Maccabee had conquered the Syrian armies and recaptured the *Beis Hamikdash.* Inside, there was a frantic search. Pure oil was needed to kindle the *Menorah,* but there was no pure oil to be found in the entire *Beis Hamikdash* because the Syrians had made everything impure. Suddenly someone found Shezazkile's flask and brought it before Yehudah. When Yehudah looked at the little flask, he said, *"Baruch Hashem,* this oil is certainly pure because the *Kohen Gadol's* seal has not been broken. But is this all the oil you could find? We will not be able to have any more oil for at least eight days. This little flask is only capable for burning for one day at the most."

Shezazkile thought to himself, "Just let them try me, I'll show them!"

After thinking awhile Yehudah said, "Use the oil, let it burn as long as it can."

When Shezazkile heard that his dream would finally come true, a strange spirit came over him. They poured him into the *Menorah* and it burned for one whole day. But strangely enough, it did not go out. It burned another, and then another day. Seven days passed, and the oil still burned. Finally, after eight days, when new oil was brought into the *Beis Hamikdash,* Shezazkile burned out. And as the light was leaving him, he had a smile on his lips for finally he had succeeded in accomplishing all that he had wanted in his life.

Now that you have heard Shezazkile's story, aren't you curious about his odd name?

Shezazkile [שֶׁזַזְכְּל] is taken from the initials of the words used by the Torah to describe the oil for the *Menorah:* שֶׁמֶן זַיִת זָךְ כָּתִית לַמָּאוֹר — Pure olive oil beaten for light.

Saved by the Rain

by Sheindel Weinbach

"**I**ma," Yehudit called out to her mother, as she entered the house returning from school. "Can I make the *sufganiyot (latkes)* tonight? *Morah* Dinah taught us how and I promise I'll be careful!"

"All right," *Geveret* (Mrs.) Shimoni replied, "but first check to see if you have everything on hand. Prepare the dough now so that you can fry the doughnuts just before we light the candles. Then we can all sit around tonight and enjoy them while we watch the candles burn."

Yehudit removed her notebook from her schoolbag and hurried into the kitchen.

"Let's see now," she muttered under her breath. "Flour — here in the canister. Salt, baking powder — in the cupboard. Two eggs — right.

"Measure … sift … deep fry … hmmm. I'll need plenty of oil for that. We're pretty low — I'd better run down to the *makolet* (grocery) and get some."

Yehudit took her shopping basket and started for the grocery. She thought back to today's lesson and recalled how *Morah* Dinah had explained about the *nes hashemen* (the miracle of oil). That little bit of oil — enough for only one day — had miraculously lasted all eight days.

"*Yeladot,*" Morah Dinah had then asked, "if there was indeed sufficient oil for one day, then the miracle only took place during the *extra* seven days that it burned. Why then do we celebrate eight days, and not seven? Go home and think about it tonight, and maybe the first *Chanukah* candle will reveal its secret."

Morah Dinah had also explained the *minhag* (custom) of eating *latkes*.

"What we call *latkes* here in *Eretz Yisrael* — jelly doughnuts — has a different meaning altogether in other lands. In Europe and America it means potato pancakes. You see, potatoes used to be scarce at this time of year in *Eretz Yisrael,* so people made flour pancakes instead. Since they are both made with plenty of oil, they are both suitable, and either kind of *latkes,* or *sufganiyot,* commemorates the *nes hashemen.*"

Yehudit had by now reached the *makolet* and was being waited on.

"*Bakbuk shemen zayit zach, bevakashah* (a jar of pure olive oil, please)," she requested from the storekeeper.

He handed her the bottle of olive oil and charged it to the Shimoni account.

Yehudit took the shortcut home, dodging puddles that formed from the morning rainfall. Suddenly she stopped short, stooped down, and picked up a lady's handbag.

"Who could have lost this, I wonder? It looks expensive. I bet it contains a lot of money. I'll bring it to the *mishtarah* (police station) tomorrow on my way to school. Whoever lost it will probably check there," she thought.

She picked up the handbag and put it in her basket, and hurried on.

Tick, tock, tick, tock …

Yehudit, deep in thought, did not hear the ominous ticking coming from the pocketbook. She entered the house, put the bottle of oil on the table, and pushed the basket with its contents into the corner where her schoolbag hung on its hook. That way she would re-member to take it along with her when she went to school the next day.

Now she busied herself with the dough, following the instructions her teacher had given her.

"Yehudit! Hurry up, honey. You still have to prepare the *chanuki-yah (menorah)* for *Abba* and Yossi," called her mother from the bedroom where she was busy dressing the baby. "It's beginning to get dark and they'll be home shortly."

Yehudit stepped out to the balcony adjoining the living room that faced the busy street. She walked over to the table and opened the glass doors of the metal box that housed the *chanukiyah,* which consisted of a single, colored whiskey glass. Filled with oil, it would burn for three hours. She filled it carefully with olive oil, and then poured a drop on her hands. She took the piece of cotton that her mother had prepared. She now rubbed her hands together to form a thin twisted thread for the wick, which she slipped into the glass. She looked at all the other balconies on the block and noticed that many families also had the same metal and glass container with its funny chimneys that enabled the lights to burn without blowing out. Of course, many people lit their *chanukiyah* on the inside window sill but her father, who still remembered the *Chanukah* he had celebrated in '48 during the blackouts of the War of Independence, wished to have his *chanukiyah* as conspicuous as possible to proclaim *Hashem's* miracles to all.

"It's not only for the great wonders that we must thank Him," he told his family year after year. "We must thank *Hashem* for every moment that we are alive, and can continue to fulfill His *mitzvos*. The *Chanukah* lights must continue to burn inside us to remind us of *Hashem's* daily miracles as well."

Yehudit placed the *shamash* candle in the special compartment on top of the metal box and closed the glass door. Then she went into the kitchen to fry her doughnuts. The small balls of dough puffed up in the sizzling oil and turned over dizzily as they continued browning on all sides. Yehudit removed them one by one from the pot and put in a new batch. While these were frying she quickly filled the first ones with her favorite strawberry jelly, sprinkled them with powdered sugar, and put them aside to cool.

Just as she had finished she heard her father and brother coming up the steps.

"*Ima*, Yehudit," *Abba* called out. "Is everything ready? I brought along a guest who has only ten minutes to spare."

Mrs. Shimoni hurried to the door to greet the guest, Channan, who was wearing the khaki outfit and green beret of the *Haganik* — *Haganah Ezrachit,* or civil defense patrol.

"*Shalom,*" he said to her. "I really only have a ten minute break now before I must hurry back to duty. Headquarters gave us specific instructions to watch out today for suspicious characters in this neighborhood. Some Arab youths who may belong to the P.L.O. have been seen hanging around lately."

Geveret Shimoni led the way to the balcony, then hurried to the bedroom to fetch the baby. *Adon* (Mr.) Shimoni insisted that everyone be present at candle lighting.

"*… sheasah nissim la'avoteinu … shehecheyanu …*"

"Now come into the warm kitchen," invited *Geveret* Shimoni when they had finished, "and taste some of my daughter's *sufganiyot* before you go back on patrol."

They all sat around the table munching the delicious doughnuts and watching the flame outside shed a lovely glow on the colored glass in the box.

Tick, tock, tick, tock …

Channan the *Haganik* took a look at his watch and looked around for the kitchen clock to check its accuracy.

"What's that ticking?" he asked in alarm. "You have no clock here in the kitchen."

Suddenly he spied the shopping basket. "What's that?" he asked, pointing to the handbag sticking out of the basket in the corner of the room. He got up to examine it, for the ticking sound clearly came from that corner.

"Quick! Everyone clear out! This is a *p'tzatzat-z'man* — a time-bomb!"

He pushed everyone out of the house and ran down to the station to fetch a demolition expert. Meanwhile a crowd gathered and everyone was asking all kinds of questions.

Channan returned with an officer, shoved his way through the crowd and ran up the stairs and into the kitchen. Everyone waited downstairs with bated breath. Soon the two men came down laughing.

"Boy, you sure have *mazal* that it rained today," said the officer. "This *p'tzatzah* (bomb) must have been placed here before the rain we had late this morning. The water did not affect the timing mechanism, but the dampness did reach the explosives inside. Why, you could have been killed if it had gone off at six, as scheduled."

The excitement died down and the crowd dispersed. The Shimoni family went back upstairs to finish the doughnuts.

"Do you realize what has happened to us, children?" asked *Adon* Shimoni of his family. "We have been saved from certain death by the rain, as the captain said. Rain — a common natural occurrence, sent by *Hashem's hashgachah* at the right time and at the right place, but nevertheless a wonderful miracle." He paused for a moment. "Actually," he continued, "the rain is no less a miracle, my children, when it causes things to grow in the fields. Every natural thing in this world is a miracle, too. Why, the very fact that our *Chanukah* wick burns the oil and sheds light is also a miracle. You may have learned, dear children, the story of Rabbi Chanina ben Dosa's daughter who, one *Erev Shabbos,* had no oil in the house for *Shabbos* lights. "Vinegar is all we have in the house," she sobbed to her saintly father, "and it is already too late to get oil."

"Go and light the vinegar," he told her. "He Who commanded oil to burn can also make vinegar burn."

"And not only did the vinegar burn," concluded *Adon* Shimoni, "but it lasted throughout the *Shabbos* and it even was used for *Havdalah*."

* * *

That night, Yehudit lay in bed, too excited to sleep. Suddenly she sat up.

"I have the answer to *Morah* Dinah's question about the eighth day. We must celebrate the very fact that oil burns at all. We must realize that all the natural things that we take for granted are also miracles."

Yehudit lay down again and fell into a deep, sweet sleep, dreaming of doughnuts and handbags and olive oil and vinegar.

The Chanukah Conspiracy

*(Based on true experiences of survivors of
the Dachau Concentration Camp)*

by A. Schreiber

Was it yesterday or two days ago that the guard shot Horowitz for trying to escape?

It was so hard to keep track of time, thought Mordechai Ansbacher, as he trudged towards Barracks #4 of the work detail in the Dachau Concentration Camp.

Days and nights, weeks and months all blurred into one aching mass. He knew only from the bitter cold in the air and the shortness of the day that winter was near.

Suddenly old Mr. Fishoff brushed by and whispered hoarsely: *"Chanukah! Chanukah!* You have just one week to *Chanukah.* Start preparing now for *Chanukah."*

One of the miracles of the Dachau Camp was the way Mr. Fishoff, who had served as *shammos* (caretaker) in the *Altneu Shul* of Prague for so many years, could continue his holy tasks in the middle of the horrors of the labor camp. Now Mr. Fishoff continued that miracle by keeping track of the passing of each and every day, and as a loyal servant of the "congregation," he was telling everyone that *Chanukah* was near.

After the men entered their barrack, they waited until the Nazi guard passed safely out of sight, and then they huddled in a corner.

"Next week is *Chanukah,*" repeated old Mr. Fishoff. "There are only seven days left to prepare."

"Prepare?" asked a young, haggard fellow from Vilna. "How can we prepare? You say there is a week left. What could we do in five weeks? Are there candles here for us, or oil?"

Mr. Fishoff ignored the pessimistic remarks. "Tomorrow," he whispered, "is Margarine Day."

Everyone knew what that meant. Once a week the prisoners of Dachau each received one dab of margarine — enough to butter one piece of dark bread. Each one treasured this little square of fat as a reminder of the comforts they all used to take for granted at home, before Dachau. More important, the fats from this cherished bit of margarine provided them each with extra fuel — extra body heat — to carry them through the entire week of grueling labor.

No one felt strong enough to part with his weekly margarine portion, but who could refuse?

"All right," said Aharon Krumbein, "you will have my

margarine. All ten grams will be yours for *Chanukah*. I am sure everyone will do the same."

Everyone nodded. Somehow — for the sake of the *mitzvah* of the *Chanukah* lights — they would last one week without the little white square.

"But how," continued Aharon, "and where will we hide it for one full week?"

Silence and pessimism again blanketed the group, for there was no secret refrigerator, no secret cooling cabinet in their bare wooden barracks.

"Here!" said Mordechai Ansbacher suddenly, shattering their silence. He pulled two large potatoes out of a brown sack where he kept personal papers and momentos. He held the potatoes aloft. "In these we will keep our margarine. I took these raw potatoes from the kitchen last week. I will hollow them out and we can store the *shemen* (oil) for our *Chanukah* light inside them."

Old Mr. Fishoff's face lit up with joy. "Very good, Mordechai," he said. "Remember now … Tomorrow!" he admonished. The group broke up, with hope and fear filling the heart of each member of the *Chanukah* conspiracy.

The next morning when the food rations for the day were handed out, each member of the work force received a piece of dark brown bread with a square of margarine on it. Most of the men spread it on the bread with their fingers or with a stick and devoured it hungrily — but not the men from Barracks #4. Each man from #4 slipped past Mordechai Ansbacher and brushed the margarine off the bread, onto a growing mound of fatty mass inside a potato. Whatever remnant stuck to the bread was hungrily enjoyed, and the two potatoes full of margarine were hidden carefully in Mordechai's sack.

Was it really a full week that passed, or only six days — or eight perhaps? Mr. Fishoff knew — and anyone who looked at him could not fail to recognize it. That night was a most special night. His very eyes shone like two bright candles, and his skin seemed to reflect a light that had its source in one of the higher worlds — a world far from the barbed wire enclosure of Dachau.

Then, as a final reminder, while the work force marched from the shops toward the barracks, Mr. Fishoff kept humming snatches of *Maoz Tzur Yeshuasi.* Yes, that night was indeed *Chanukah,* and no one had a doubt but that the old *shammos* himself would kindle the lights.

When the guard passed beyond Barracks #4, the members of the conspiracy huddled around the old man expectantly. He motioned toward Ansbacher, and the men made an opening in the small crowd for him to pass through with his valuable cargo.

"I have the oil," he said, "but what will we use for a *menorah?*"

"Don't worry. Don't worry," said the old man, his face beaming with happiness. "The potatoes you used for storage will serve us well as a *menorah.* We have nothing better, and this way we will not lose a drop. Now disperse. It is not safe yet. Come back at midnight, when the guards change."

The men slipped back to their places. At midnight the "sleeping" men of Barracks #4 suddenly all "awoke" at once and gathered around old Mr. Fishoff. He held a lit match up high as he pronounced the *brachos.*

The men answered *amen* to his blessings and together with him declared: הַנֵּרוֹת הַלָּלוּ קוֹדֶשׁ הֵם — "these lamps are holy." They did not witness only a lighting of a *menorah* in a concentration camp. They were transported miles and months away. Some thought they were back in the *Altneu Shul* in Prague witnessing their beloved *shammos* kindling the *menorah.*

When the men crawled back into their places to sleep, they dreamed that they were in Jerusalem two thousand years earlier, watching the *Kohen* kindle oil lamps of a new *Menorah* in a rededicated *Beis Hamikdash.*

Five hours later the men of Barracks #4 were awakened from their sleep. The working day in Dachau was beginning. They marched out to their tasks charged with a new warmth and vitality. This extra energy was from margarine that was burning — but not within their bodies. It was burning and warming them from within their souls.

Menorah in the Window

by Rabbi Elchonon (Charles) Wengrov

Miracles really happen. Some we see and some we don't. Come let me tell you about a miracle that I saw happen just last night. But maybe I'd better start from the beginning.

* * *

The first time I saw him he was running. It seemed suspicious; a young kid — alone — running at night through the forest of a deserted, ruined German town. I called out to him to halt. He ran even faster. Then he dropped behind a tree and lay still, figuring I couldn't find him in the dark. After you've been a soldier in the U.S. army during a war, you know a couple of tricks. I stood in place, moving my feet up and down, but my footsteps sounded in the forest exactly as if I were going back to the center of town. Then I waited, as silent as the night.

The kid started out again, quietly, looking around to make sure he was alone. I followed, without a sound. Near the edge of the forest he stopped, looked around carefully, and got to his knees. With his fingers he loosened the earth around a big rock. He lifted the big stone with all his strength, and rolled it aside. His fingers scooped the earth in the hole, faster and faster. Then he was tugging at something … at last he lifted it out.

"All right, son. Let's have it." My voice was stern and I shone

my flashlight full on him. He tried to run again, but I caught him in a minute. "It's mine, it's mine!" he shouted in terror. "You can't take it from me." He was badly frightened, but he wouldn't cry. None of these youngsters who had lived through the Nazi regime could cry any more. It was then that I noticed what he was holding — a beautiful *menorah.*

"All right, all right, son," I said. "I won't hurt you. Just sit down and tell me about it. Here — here's a chocolate bar."

He kept trying to run away from me. After the Nazis, he was scared of anyone wearing a uniform. But I held on to him, and finally he gave up trying. He ate the chocolate — he was starved — but he kept looking at me as though he was wondering when I'd hit him. I did everything I could to make him feel safe. Finally he relaxed. And he told me his story.

The *menorah* was a family heirloom — something that had gone from father to son for a couple of hundred years. Well, before the Nazis started arresting all the Jews, his father went and buried the *menorah,* and the boy memorized the spot. Among the last things his father told him was "Try to get the *menorah.* Keep it, for with it our family serves *Hashem* on *Chanukah."* The boy remembered the exact words.

"Where's your father now?" I asked him.

"The Nazis shot him." Just like that he said it. No crying. Just a pain in his eyes.

"And your mother?" I asked gently.

"I don't know." He just sat by my side, staring. Right then and there I made up my mind. "Look," I said, "how would you like me to be your big brother? I'll take care of you; later we'll go to America."

"America ..." he repeated the word as if in a dream, something far away, beautiful.

"What's your name?" I asked him.

"David," he answered in a trusting voice.

David stayed with me. I had a tough time getting my superior officers to okay it, but he stayed with me. And he kept that *menorah* by his side.

A long time after that, I was sent home. The army didn't want me any more. I filled out a lot of papers, and David came with me. He looked a little better now, thanks to all the milk and chocolate and vitamins I'd been able to get for him. We went home.

In no time at all David was a regular member of the family. My mother took very good care of him, and my Dad liked to talk Yiddish with him — it reminded Dad of the old country. David went to a *yeshivah* day school, learned English, learned baseball, and in short — he was doing fine. It took a long time, but he even learned to laugh.

Then the art expert came.

Mr. Okun works in a Jewish museum in New York. Once a year he visits his sister in our city, and then he always pays us a visit, because he and my Dad are old friends.

This year my Dad had something new to show Mr. Okun — my "kid brother" David. David was upstairs in his room doing homework, so we went up. We entered, and David looked up.

"David," said my Dad, "I want you to meet an old friend of mine, Mr. Okun."

"How do you do?" said David.

Mr. Okun asked him the usual questions, and the young fellow answered everything politely. Then Mr. Okun happened to see David's *menorah* on the dresser, bright and shining. You should've seen Mr. Okun. His eyes almost popped.

"Where does *this* come from?" he cried. "A genuine thirteenth century German *menorah!* Why, this must be the only one of its kind in the world! Very unusual design!" Then Mr. Okun had to stop for breath, and he came down to earth. "Er, whose is it?"

"It's mine, sir," said David.

"You must sell it to me," Mr. Okun went on. "You must sell it to the Jewish museum. I'll give you fifty thousand dollars for it. Why it's a work of art ... it's priceless ..."

Mr. Okun kept talking. I guess he liked the sound of his voice. But David was badly frightened. In his eyes was the same look as I'd seen that night in the forest when I had tried to take the *menorah* from him. He was afraid again. Someone was trying to take the *menorah* from him again.

I leaned down and whispered, "David, you don't have to give him the *menorah*. It's yours. This is America — a free country." He looked at me, still afraid, and I held his hand. He calmed down.

"I don't want to sell it, sir." Calmly, he said it. Just like that.

Mr. Okun wouldn't give up. He spoke beautifully about what you can do with fifty thousand bucks. Then he took another look at David's face, and he quieted down. A kid who's gone through a concentration camp can be stubborn as a rock. David was stubborn now. He was whispering to himself. "Try to get the *menorah*. Keep it, for with it our family serves *Hashem* on *Chanukah*" — his father's last words.

The next day was terrific. The newspapers heard about it. They wanted pictures of the *menorah* and of David — and they wanted the full story of a kid who threw away fifty thousand real, honest-to-goodness dollars. The story made the network news broadcasts, and the Sunday feature sections. It didn't bother David. People all over the country wrote letters to him. It didn't bother David. He had his *menorah*.

The months went by, and *Chanukah* came. My Dad did as usual. He put his tin *menorah* on the mantelpiece and lit the first candle. Not so David. He put his *menorah* on the window sill, made sure the curtains wouldn't catch fire, and lit *his* first candle. "That's the way it's supposed to be," said David, "so that everyone can see it." Then he went into the kitchen to watch the *laktes* sizzling on the fire.

It was quiet in the dining room. Just my Dad and I were sitting around, smoking our pipes. The candles flickered. Then there was a knock on the door. I went to open it. A middle-aged woman stood there.

"Pardon me," she said in a broken, halting English. "May I ask you something?"

"Surely," I said, "but won't you come in?"

She stood inside the doorway and pointed at David's *menorah*. "I see that *menorah* in your window. How did you get that? It is very funny. In my family, in Europe, there was one just like that … just, just the same. It was a … how do you say it … a

family heirloom, you know? It is funny. How did you get that? I
didn't think that there was another like it in the whole world. It is
funny, no? I hope that you will excuse me for asking you."

I looked at her closely. And a strange, crazy thought entered my head. Was it possible? She looked a little like ...

"Just a moment," I said, and I went into the kitchen. "David," I said, "go into the living room."

I watched from the kitchen door. David looked at her, and she looked at him. Then he was in her arms, crying, "Mamma, Mamma, Mamma ..." He was crying — for the first time in years ... and so was I.

In the window, the *menorah* stood, proudly watching.

A Ray of Light

by Nechama Rosenbaum

Izzy couldn't remember ever feeling so lost and alone. It was early December, a damp, cold mist covered the Belgian farmlands, and he wished he was back home in Pittsburgh instead of fighting Nazis in Europe. He sat up on his army cot, picked up a piece of paper, and started to scribble a note to his parents:

Dear Folks,

It's a rotten war, and I wish we never got mixed up in it. My buddy Sol, whom I wrote you about, was shot in the shoulder yesterday, and is laid up in the hospital.

I'm getting jittery myself, and I don't know why I can't be home with you. But don't worry, I'll get out of this one way or another.

Regards to all my friends who are still left.

Your son,

Isidore

Mike, the top sergeant, passed through the barracks, and stopped in front of Izzy's bed. He looked at him intently and seemed to read in his sagging face the gloomy message of the letter.

"Izzy-boy," he said, "you look like you've had too much shooting war. Why not go into the village for the afternoon? You don't have to be back until the night curfew. It'll do you good."

"Village?" scoffed Izzy. "That's no village. It's just four farmhouses, with a square in the middle for some old statue. Besides, no one there speaks a word of English and I don't know any Flemish."

Izzy did not wait for an answer, though, and began to change from his fatigues to a dress uniform. In five minutes he was walking smartly down the road that ran along an old canal to the village, dodging around bomb craters and piles of bricks that interrupted the road's course. Whenever a plane passed overhead, Izzy involuntarily ducked into a ditch on the farther side of the road, as though the planes overhead were Nazi, not American.

Once he reached the village square, he found the people scurrying in all directions. In a few more minutes it would be five o'clock, and the curfew, with lights out and shades drawn, would begin.

"What can I do?" Izzy asked himself. "Everyone has a place to go, a home where he belongs. I'm all alone here. No one wants me in his house — and even if they did, I can't speak a word of their language, anyway."

He settled down on a cold stone bench, lit up a cigarette and watched the last few people slip into their houses and lock their doors behind them — locking him out. No lights showed through the shattered windows, and a jet-black moonless night was descending on the little village. In a small, stone house at the edge of the square a shutter hung loosely on its hinges and Izzy caught sight of a flickering candle ... The light seemed to be moving slowly, bobbing up and down, then suddenly increasing

by one, then another, and another.

Out of curiosity, Izzy stole closer to the window. The flickering candle seemed to remind him of something from the distant past, but he could not recall what. He peered into the window. A family was gathered around a brass candleholder, and Izzy could detect a faint tune of joy drifting through the smothering silence.

Footsteps in the cobblestone distance. "I've gotta get out of here," mumbled Izzy, "before that watchman catches me here after nightfall."

He turned to go, but first he carefully lifted the heavy wooden shutter back in place and shut out the tender scene from his view.

Suddenly he heard a sharp "Pssst." Izzy looked to the doorway to his right. Two large eyes glistened in the dark. He stepped toward them cautiously and found that they belonged to a small girl, perhaps nine years old, with long, black, braided hair.

"*Merci, Monsieur American,*" she whispered, and motioned him into the house.

"I can't go in," he argued, "I'll be late for mess." But his feet still took him into the narrow doorway, after the little girl.

"I must be *meshuga* (crazy) to do this," he added.

The girl stopped and looked at him. "*Zent Ihr a Yid* (are you a Jew)?" she asked, and without waiting for a reply, she rushed into the first room off the corridor, and spoke quickly and excitedly to the people inside. A grey-haired, mustached man stepped forward with his arms extended toward Izzy. He embraced him warmly, and told him in halting English, "Welcome, American soldier, to our home. You saved us from certain danger by closing the shutter. In our excitement over *Chanukah,* we forgot to keep the light inside. It could have meant much trouble … Sit down and enjoy our holiday feast with us."

Chanukah! So that's it, thought Izzy. I haven't heard that word since I studied for my *bar mitzvah* in Hebrew School, seven years ago.

"I must return to my regiment," said Izzy, but when the mother of the home came into the room with a tray full of steaming fragrant *latkes,* Izzy forgot his protests, and sat down next to the father of the group. He picked up a *latke* with a fork and held it for a moment.

"*Baruch atah* … You know, if you helped me with the right *brachah,*" Izzy said, "I might remember how to say it."

"So you are Jewish," the father beamed. He embraced Izzy once more. After he helped him with the *brachah,* he began to speak excitedly, sometimes forgetting himself and speaking French, other times throwing in a Yiddish word; still the story came through.

"This is our first *Chanukah* in five years. We have been in hiding in a farm nearby since Hitler came to power — but we could not show that we were Jewish or it would have been the end. Every holiday was like *Tishah B'Av* because it only seemed to make us remember how deep our *galus* (exile) was. We did not celebrate and sing last *Chanukah.* We cried because we had no *menorah,* no oil, no candles — only darkness."

He sighed for a moment, and everyone else in the room echoed the sound of despair from the horrible years gone by.

"But we did not give up hope. You know how the Maccabees were few and weak, and the enemy was strong and many? Still *Hashem* came to their rescue. We, too, were so few and so weak, and the Nazis were evil, many, and strong; but we knew that the *yeshuah* (help) would come."

The man smiled a moment, and then added, "And here you are."

Izzy was embarrassed by the attention he was getting. Just a few hours before he was cursing the war and wishing himself home, and now he was being given a hero's welcome and getting all the credit for a war he only wanted to escape.

The man sensed his discomfort. "We are so rude," he said. "We invite you in, and do not even tell you our name. I am Moshe Perlman. This is my wife, the two boys are my sons, Aaron and Benjamin; and this is my niece, Sarah."

Aaron said something in French that started them all agiggle.

"Aaron wanted you to meet his *dreidel,* also, that he carved out of beech wood last year, when we were still in hiding. I think he is right. Enough talk. Join us in a game."

Before Izzy could think, Mrs. Perlman entered again with more *latkes,* a baked apple concoction, and some buttermilk. The children set up little piles of nuts for the *dreidel* game. So Izzy took his seat again and unloaded some chocolate from one of his pockets. To the children's delight, and his own pleasure, Izzy lost all of his squares of chocolate to his three competitors. A kettle boiled happily, light and gay talk floated in from the kitchen, and laughter and exaggerated moaning surrounded the *dreidel* game.

Suddenly a cuckoo clock sang out the passing of the sixth hour, and Izzy jumped to his feet. "I'm late!" he blurted out. "I've got to get out of here or it's the guardhouse for me, for sure."

The game stopped short. Everyone seemed to be holding his breath while Izzy pulled on his coat.

"*Mon ami, Izzy,*" Mr. Perlman whispered most apologetically, "you are in trouble? We have detained you, away from your duty? We are so selfish to keep you here for our pleasure, and now you have penalties to pay!"

Izzy laughed. "Don't worry, I'll be O.K. I'll tell you the truth, your friendship and the lessons you taught me would be worth a thousand days in jail."

The Perlmans looked at each other, very puzzled. "Lesson? I did not want to lecture you. How do you mean?"

"I mean, you taught me why I'm fighting — to save people like you from death and persecution. You taught me how to be brave, and you taught me ..."

Mr. Perlman moved his hand as if to cut off his words. "We taught you nothing. You gave us comfort, and you must come again tomorrow to light the *menorah* with us.

Izzy frowned. "I don't know where I'll be tomorrow. But no matter where I'll be, I'll light the *Chanukah* candles myself. And if I can't — if I must be in darkness at the battle lines — I'll shut my eyes and pretend I'm with you. That way I'll have hope for light, the way you did these last four years, and the way the Maccabees did thousands of years back."

"And the way Jews do and have always done," Mr. Perlman added.

Izzy slipped out the door into the December cold, the Perlmans good wishes warming his ears against the blistering wind. No moon shone. Only icy blue stars gleamed in the velvet sky. He hurried along the road back to his encampment, his back to the little Belgian village.

For a few minutes he rehearsed his excuse to the lieutenant.

Are they thinking him dead, or a cowardly deserter? Well, he was neither, and his story of being lost was a good one, and partly true.

Then he began to plan lighting his own *Chanukah* candles the next night — in his bunk? In a tent somewhere? In a foxhole? He imagined questions — some teasing, some sincere — and he planned his answers.

Finally, his thoughts shifted to the next year — home in the states, he hoped. There he would find a candle of belief and trust in *Hashem,* like the Perlmans had in their years of hiding, to light up a new way of life for the rest of his years.

Don't Say Goodbye

by Rabbi Nisson Wolpin

Daniel Greenstein expected to be alone. It was the sixth night of *Chanukah,* and he was sure that the other fellows would be home with their families. His parents did not hear him leave. It also happened to be December 31, New Year's Eve, and hardly the time for a *yeshivah* boy to venture out on a stroll. It was cold and rainy, when no one would step out unless it was an emergency. This was an emergency, thought Daniel. He wanted to say good-bye to the Mesivta High School of Stratford.

Hands deep in his jacket pockets, collar up against the wind, he looked longingly at the store-front building where his ninth grade had met for the last four months. He then gazed upstairs where twelve out-of-towners had dormitory rooms ... Where would they stay when they returned from their *Chanukah* vacation?

"Hey, Danny! You're late for our night-*seder* (Torah study session)."

Daniel whirled around. Behind him were Yehudah Schwartz and Velvy Rosen. Another figure was crossing into view from the other side of Washington Avenue. It was his own *chavrusa* (study companion), Chaim Berger.

"I'm glad you can still joke, Yehudah. I find losing our Mesivta building tragic," Daniel muttered.

"I don't know what the rush is," Velvy said. "They can't put up new buildings until Spring anyway. Why can't we stay until then?"

"Urban Renewal waits for nothing," explained Yehudah. "January 1st, pfft! Out we go … January 2nd — wham! Wrecking ball begins to swing … January 12 — vroom! The trucks drive up, and …"

"Stop it already," shouted Daniel.

"Hi, fellows!" It was Chaim, with a comforting word as usual. "I have the key to our old building. Why bid a frigid farewell to our *makom kadosh* (holy place)? Let's go inside. It is still ours for another hundred and fifty minutes."

Chaim put down some packages, unlocked the door and swung it open, and switched on the light. The room was bare. All the desks and books had been moved to the Stratford Hebrew Day School cellar that afternoon. Only two benches stood along one of the walls. The boys shuddered.

Chaim whipped out a *Chanukah menorah* from one bag and set it on the window sill. He stuck in six candles and lit them. Next he pulled out some cake, unfolded some foil-wrapped steaming *latkes,* and uncorked two soda bottles.

"You're amazing!" breathed Velvy.

"Chaim! How can you think of food at a time like this?" Daniel sputtered.

"Chaim thinks of food all the time," Yehudah quipped.

"Especially on *Chanukah,*" chuckled Chaim. "It's a holiday, so let's not make a mourning fast out of an evening feast. A bite and some *Chanukah* celebrating might give our sinking spirits a lift."

He set out five portions of refreshments as he hummed a *Chanukah* tune. Daniel begrudgingly joined his feasting friends, and pointed at the fifth plate. "Who's that for? Anyway, how did you know we were coming?"

"Last things first: You're here, aren't you?" retorted Chaim. "And as for the fifth, that's for ..."

"Me," said Rabbi Feinberg as he slammed the door shut.

His four *talmidim* (students) jumped up, half from respect and half from being startled.

"You boys really shouldn't be out on a night like this," said Rabbi Feinberg. "But I guess I can't blame you. After all, here I am for the very same reason," he added with a sigh.

Rabbi Feinberg sat on the one bench with his *talmidim* and picked up his plate of *latkes* from the other bench. He paused for a minute. "You know, boys, this is almost the worst day in my life."

"Almost?" asked Daniel. "What could have ever been worse? After all the trouble you went to — moving from New York, finding students from other communities to join our Mesivta High School, getting our parents to consent ..."

"And getting me to agree," added Yehudah.

Daniel shot him his usual harsh glance, and then continued, "I can hardly think of a worse letdown than having your building condemned for Urban Renewal with no place to go. This is absolutely the worst day of *my* life."

"I said 'almost,' Daniel, for one reason. Your *Chanukah* candles in the window reminded me of darker days that I never lived through, of threats more final than a building being shut down. Yet our people survived and were even victorious. I say 'almost' because this day is not yet over."

The boys stared at the flickering candles, and looked out the window into the black night. Two slightly drunk men passed by laughing and shoving each other. Hope seemed very far away.

Chaim shattered the gloom by breaking into a song: "Yevanim, Yevanim, nikbetzu alie ..." *Those Greeks ganged up on us in the days of the Chashmonaim. They broke the walls ... defiled the oil. From a left-over jug a miracle happened ... Wise men established eight days for song and joy.*

They all joined voices in singing. Things *were* worse once. The Greeks weren't just interested in beautifying their streets. They wanted to change our religion. Our people had to fight for very basic things — Torah study, keeping holidays, *bris milah.* The sides were uneven, with strength and numbers with the enemy. Even when we won, we couldn't light our *menorah* in the *Beis Hamikdash* because we did not have enough pure oil. But we did it, and that one flask lasted eight days. Never despair. Always have hope. We are children of the *Chashmonaim.*

"Yevanim, Yevanim ..." they sang again and again, and the same thoughts ran through five minds like a broad stream of strength.

"Boy, I'd like to get my hands on that Jack Maslo of the City Construction Council. He's definitely one of those *Yevanim,*" said Yehudah.

"Don't say that!" interrupted Chaim. "Don't you know his father, old Mr. Maslovsky, who reads the Torah in the Downtown *Shul?*"

"That's his father?"

"You mean he's Jewish?"

"Well, I'll be …!"

Rabbi Feinberg seemed lost in thought. *So Jack Maslo is Mr. Maslovsky's son. We'll have to daven in the Downtown Shul tomorrow.*

"Boys," he said aloud, "let's clean up. This building may be the home of the Mesivta of Stratford for just a little while longer. It's too soon to say goodbye."

* * *

There were five guests at the eight o'clock *minyan* at the *Beis Haknesses Anshei Shalom* of Stratford, better known as the Downtown *Shul,* and they completed the *minyan.* At the reading of the Torah, Mr. Maslovsky presided like a Prime Minister at Parliament, and he made sure that all of the guests were honored with *aliyos, hagba'ah,* and *glillah.*

"How did you know we needed you for a *minyan?*" Mr. Maslovsky asked Rabbi Feinberg after *Shacharis.*

"One Jew knows when another is in need," he answered with a smile.

"True," nodded Mr. Maslovsky. "And what is your problem?"

"Aha! You feel my ache in your heart, too," the rabbi said. "My problem is that I need time."

"Ah, don't we all yearn for more time? *Halevai,* I only wish I could grant you what you need."

"You cannot help me, but your son can. If we could see him today, we might be able to get what we need."

"We?"

"Yes, I and my *talmidim* of the Mesivta. Can you arrange it?"

"Arrange it?" the old man snorted. "I'll take you there myself!"

Fifteen minutes later Mr. Maslovsky's car came to a stop alongside a brick colonial home in suburban Stratford Hills. The four boys and Mr. Maslovsky hopped out of the car, but Rabbi Feinberg hesitated. "Are you sure it's not too early?" he asked.

"Of course not. I call on him anytime. I *am* his father."

He rang the bell. A man in a lounging robe answered the door. "Pa! What are you doing here? Is something wrong?"

The older man just walked in. "Never mind is something wrong, Yankel. Invite in your guests."

The "guests" and the "host" just looked at each other. Finally, he motioned them into a spacious living room.

"You're driving them out of their building, Yankel. The Mesivta is closing. Change it!" the old man ordered.

"Wait, Pa. I don't know what you mean. Anyway, can't this wait? It's 9:00 A.M. and I've hardly ..."

"It's just like I said," Yehudah whispered too loudly. "He's one of the *Yevanim*. We're wasting our time."

"Keep quiet!" said Daniel desperately.

"Wait!" protested Mr. Maslo. "What did he call me?"

"Nothing, really," Rabbi Feinberg said nervously.

"I said you're like the Syrian-Greeks of centuries ago who plagued our people and wouldn't allow them to keep the Torah. And you seem to be proving it more by the minute!"

"Believe me, I don't know what you are talking about. I'd

like to throw you out of my house, but first tell me what you're accusing me of being."

"Please forgive the boys," Rabbi Feinberg said, "but they are extremely upset. Our *yeshivah* has been meeting in a storefront on Washington Avenue. Urban Renewal has marked our building for demolition, and we have no place to go. It's simply the end of our high school."

"And you could delay it for a half year if you wanted to. It's just that you put beauty ahead of Torah, like the *Yevanim!*" Yehudah blurted out.

His friends looked on in horror at his burst of temper.

"Now see here, young man," Mr. Maslo said in deep

earnestness. "I am a loyal Jew, and respect Torah. I studied in afternoon Hebrew school as a kid. That's all we had then. I don't want to see your school close down, but we've got a schedule to keep. The land must be clear by the time the freeze is over."

"So, what's the rush?"

"True, we could spare two or three weeks, but where would you go then?" Mr. Maslo asked.

He began pacing the long carpeted floor. Suddenly he stopped and whirled around. "I have it!" he shouted with excitement. "The old Battalion Hall has been abandoned since June and is scheduled to go down next summer. Why not transfer classes there?"

Mr. Maslo cleared his throat. "Of course, I don't run the City Construction Council. I'm only the Chairman. But I'm sure the others will see things my way. After all, education is of utmost importance. Only ..."

"Yes?" everyone asked in unison.

"Remember, I'm not one of the *Yevanim*. I light a real *menorah* in my study room in the north of the house ... Have me in mind in your studies, and I'll have you in mind in the City Council Chambers tomorrow."

Victory after so many days of despair was more than the boys could contain. They all started talking and gesturing at once. Rabbi Feinberg finally extended his hand to Jack "Yankel" Maslo.

"Don't say goodbye," Mr. Maslo said. "We will have to meet again and again. From this one meeting I hope that we can get together and accomplish much more. Maybe even eight times as much," he added, with a twinkle in his eye.

Mysteries and Miracles

by Sarah Birnhack

"**F**raidy, clear those books off your dresser and come down — you're late for school!" called Mrs. Weber as she finished putting breakfast on the table. Fraidy hurried into the dinette and slid breathlessly into her chair.

"Oh Mommy, I'm sorry I'm late again! I know you wanted to get an early start today because Carmela is coming to do the cleaning, but I just *had* to finish the last chapter of my library book.

"I don't have time to wash ... I'll just have some cereal and juice."

"Fraidy, this has got to stop, you know. You're forever with your nose in a library book and it's not fair. I wish you'd spend more time with Debby. You know it's hard for her. Before she came you were always begging for a sister and now ... I thought it would be different."

Just then Debby Rosen came into the dinette ready for school. She was eleven, the same age as Fraidy, and had come to the Webers as a foster child in September. Fraidy had wanted to love her as a sister, but when she had asked her mother about Debby's background, Mrs. Weber had not answered her.

"Don't ever ask Debby anything, you hear, Fraidy? Just be her friend and forget about her past."

Fraidy had tried, but somehow it hadn't worked out too well. Now Debby was waiting patiently for Fraidy to finish her juice. Fraidy kissed her mother and ran out with Debby into the snowy December day.

As she and Debby walked to school they discussed the class party where they had raised $65 to buy toys as *Chanukah* gifts for children in the hospital. As class treasurer, Fraidy was in charge of the money and she would go shopping with her teacher for the toys.

"Oh, Fraidy, look! It's still there!" called Debby as she ran to the window of the antique shop. Every day for the last week,

Debby had looked longingly at a small bronze *menorah* displayed in the window.

"I don't blame you for wanting it — it's really beautiful — but why do you need a *menorah* anyway? Come on, it's late."

And they hurried off.

The day was a happy one for Fraidy and it passed quickly. But by the time Fraidy returned home she was in despair.

"What's wrong?" exclaimed Mrs. Weber when she saw her daughter's tear-streaked face.

Fraidy dropped her briefcase, flung her coat onto a chair and herself onto the couch. She broke into sobs. "It's the money! Oh Mommy, the money's gone. When it came time to pay for the toys I couldn't find it. Mrs. Scheinman paid for them but I've got to pay her back. I know I put it in my purse. I'm sure I had it with me when I went to school — and now it's gone!"

Fraidy couldn't continue talking. Her whole being was troubled. She was sure she'd never forget her fear and humiliation. She'd never be the same again!

Debby and the Webers searched the house, but found no trace of the missing money. Mrs. Weber called Mrs. Scheinman who was quite sure that it hadn't been stolen or lost in school. She was sorry, but Fraidy would have to replace the missing money. She hoped it would turn up soon.

The next morning, Debby left for school early since she was in the choir that was practicing for the *Chanukah* assembly. Fraidy, late again, walked alone, heavy-hearted. She was no longer treasurer of her class. She was irresponsible. Nothing she did lately was right, just like the girl in the book she was reading.

But in books there were happy endings and she couldn't foresee one for herself.

She stopped automatically to look into the window of the antique shop. She'd say hello to Debby's pet *menorah*. But to her surprise it was gone, missing. She hurried to school to tell Debby.

"The *menorah?* ... Well, I knew it wouldn't be there long ... thanks for telling me."

Fraidy was puzzled. Debby hadn't seemed surprised to hear about the *menorah*. After looking at it for more than a week she didn't seem interested. As a matter of fact it was as if she didn't want to discuss it. Hmmmm ... Fraidy wondered.

The girls in her class were very sympathetic to Fraidy that day. They each gave her a different suggestion as to what might have happened to the money and by the time she returned home she was no longer so sure that she had put it in her purse.

"Maybe I left it on my dresser or some other place around the house, Mommy. Maybe Carmela took it. I once read a book where the maid 'borrowed' the money for a sick aunt and ..."

"Fraidy, that's ridiculous. You and your books. Carmela has worked for us over a year and she's honest. You must have lost it on the way to school."

"I didn't lose it, Mommy. It's a mystery and I'm going to solve it. I just need a few clues. I'm going to my room. If you need me, call. O.K.?"

Fraidy went to her room and opened the door without knocking. Debby had been bending over the desk wrapping something. When she saw Fraidy, she grabbed the package and hid it behind her back. She ran to the closet, unlocked her suitcase, put in the package and relocked the case. Fraidy watched her silently. Debby left the room and Fraidy sat down on her bed.

Wow! This was a real mystery. First the money was missing. Then the *menorah* was gone. Then Debby was hiding something. All you had to do was add one, plus one, plus one, and you get three. Debby had taken the money to buy the *menorah!* What she wanted it for, Fraidy didn't know. Come to think of it, Fraidy didn't know anything about Debby.

"I'll get to the bottom of this," thought Fraidy. "I can solve a mystery as well as anyone in a book."

Fraidy waited for Debby to mention the hidden package and when she didn't Fraidy decided on a plan.

The next day Fraidy told her mother that she'd be late after school because she was going to the library to return some library books. She was planning to go to the library, but first she'd do a little investigating.

She made her way down the darkening streets to the antique shop. The old man who owned it refused to speak to her. "I answered enough questions about that *menorah*. Please go."

Fraidy walked to the library disappointed that her investigation yielded nothing. Maybe she wasn't such a good detective after all!

She placed her books on the counter, assured the librarian that none were overdue and rushed down the steps two at a time. Daddy would be lighting the *menorah* soon and she didn't want to be late.

When Fraidy came into the living room everyone was there,

ready for Daddy to begin. And then she saw it. Right next to Daddy's silver one, was the small bronze *menorah!*

Fraidy was about to accuse Debby when she noticed a tall stranger, half hidden by the drapes. Daddy started the *brachos* (blessings), and Fraidy listened intently. Then the stranger lit the beautiful bronze *menorah* and joined Daddy in singing *Maoz Tzur.* Fraidy noticed that both Mommy and Debby had tears in their eyes. She was as puzzled as ever.

As soon as everyone was seated, Daddy turned to Fraidy. "*Chanukah* is a time of miracles and one has just happened to us.

This is Debby's father. He's been searching for Debby without results for days and this morning he saw this *menorah* in the antique shop. He recognized it immediately, since he had received it for his *bar mitzvah* many years ago. The man who owns the shop keeps records of the people from whom he buys objects and he gave Mr. Rosen our address."

"I ... I don't understand. I mean ... I thought Debby *bought* the *menorah* and now you say that she *sold* it!"

"That's right. She wanted money to buy gifts for us, to show how much she appreciated the home we've given her. So she sold her most precious possession — the one thing that was saved when her home was destroyed by fire.

"Her father was in Europe at that time, on business, and when he heard that his family and home were wiped out, he became very ill. He was in the hospital for six months.

"As soon as he recovered he returned to America. How thankful he was to hear that Debby had survived! But no one in Woodbridge knew where she was. His friends only knew that she was someplace in New York, but they didn't know where."

Debby's father finished the story. "I kept hoping and praying for a miracle. We say, שֶׁעָשָׂה נִסִּים לַאֲבוֹתֵינוּ בַּיָּמִים הָהֵם 'בַּזְּמַן הַזֶּה' — that *Hashem* performs miracles in this time of *Chanukah* as he did in the days of the *Chashmonaim*. Now I know it's true. I bought the *menorah* and got your address from the storekeeper. So I found my Debby and my *menorah* — and Debby was able to buy gifts for all you wonderful people."

"One more piece of good news tonight!" announced Mrs. Weber as she came in from the kitchen carrying a plate of sizzling crisp *latkes*. "The librarian just called. She found an envelope with $65 in one of the books you just returned."

Fraidy was speechless. Why, this was better than any book she'd ever read! She ran to Debby and hugged her. Fraidy had a sister after all.

Hawaiian Wonder

by Ursula Lehmann

Higher and higher the waves rose. Avi Gross tried to guide his foam surfboard along their peaks before they broke. Finally, he had to admit defeat; today's waves were just too high and swift for him to ride.

Avi slipped into his terrycloth robe and ran across the warm sands of the deserted beach to a grassy terrace where his little sister, Miriam, sat waiting for him. Then he and Miriam watched the setting sun paint the Hawaiian skies a brilliant crimson.

Avi liked Hawaii more than some of the other posts where his father had been stationed. Every few years Mr. Gross was sent by the United States Parks Department to a new post somewhere else in the United States. He was one of their top forest rangers and Avi was very proud of him, but never before had he realized his good fortune in having a father who led such an interesting life as he did this year, when they were transferred to the fiftieth state.

"The only thing I'm sorry about," Avi mused to Miriam, "is that there are no other people here. Dad and Mom have their troubles getting meat and things, but at least they have that big freezer to store food in once they get it. Our problems are not so easy to solve. I learn *Gemara* with Dad every day, but it just isn't the same as studying with my friends in the *yeshivah* in Denver.

These are things we can't get flown in from the mainland and keep in a freezer."

"Well," said Miriam, "at least we can enjoy Hawaii. Just look at that sunset!"

For a moment all was quiet except for the rhythmic pounding of the surf. Then, with a happy sigh, they picked up their books and *seforim* (Hebrew books) and started home for supper.

Home was not very spacious. Kona, the island they lived on, was still rather primitive. Their house was built of wood, their electricity was created in their own generator, and their drinking water came from a well, but the scenery was beautiful and the weather was one long comfortable summer.

Avi swung his beach towel over his shoulder. He began to review in his mind the lesson he would have to report on to his father. His afternoon near the surf had not been idle. Mr. Gross had given his children assignments to do, and Avi had been busy studying *dinim* (laws) of *Chanukah* in the *seforim* that he had taken with him, while little Miriam practiced Hebrew script and memorized her multiplication tables.

"It's a funny thing," he said to Miriam, "but all these laws I learned today are pretty easy to keep, except one of the most important of them all! The *Chanukah* lights must be seen! How in the world is anyone going to see our *Chanukah* lights out here in the middle of nowhere?"

"Don't be such a worry bug," Miriam answered in exasperation. "You've got two whole weeks until *Chanukah,* and who knows what will turn up by then?"

"Oh, I know what will turn up!" Avi answered. "We'll drive 200 miles so Mom can shop and do the laundry in Hilo and *then* we'll see some people. But aside from the next laundry trip we won't see a soul, and certainly no one will see our *Chanukah* lights!"

Avi was a rather unhappy boy by the time Mr. Gross came home and prepared the table for their nightly study session. All evening Avi had been preoccupied, and his fun at the surf was almost forgotten.

"Well, what *dinim* did you find?" asked his father, as they pulled up their chairs.

"Nothing really new, I guess," answered Avi slowly. "The candles must not be more than twenty *amos* high (30-40 feet), we light them from left to right …" Avi's voice dwindled away, and he began doodling on the paper he usually kept for notes.

Mr. Gross looked up. One glance at his son told him that something was wrong. Besides that, when he came in from his day in the forest, Mrs. Gross had dropped a word of warning. "There's something bothering Avi," she began quietly. "Miriam knows what it is, but she won't say. It must be something she's afraid would hurt our feelings, otherwise she would tell us. Go a little easy with him, won't you?"

So Mr. Gross was forewarned. He closed the *Shulchan Aruch* that was open before him and turned to Avi. "What's the matter, Avi? What's on your mind?"

"It's not your fault," began Avi. "I love Hawaii and so does Miriam, but …" Avi's voice drifted off.

"But, what?" prompted Mr. Gross quietly.

"But I miss my friends, I guess," finished Avi. "Miriam and I like to meet the guests who come to see you, but it's so seldom anyone comes, and our long ride to Hilo just isn't enough. We see people in Hilo, but they're just people, not really friends. I love learning with you, Dad, but it's still not the same as being with all my *yeshivah* friends …" Avi stopped, looking aghast at what he had said.

"Of course it isn't," interrupted his father. "That's the way it should be. It's never the same learning privately as it is to learn with a group of boys. But we've been here for almost half a year now and you were never so bothered before. Something must have brought this all to mind. What is it?"

"You're right," Avi admitted. "It's those *dinim* of *Chanukah*. From my learning today I see that one of the most important laws of the *Chanukah* candles is *pirsumei nissa,* spreading the news of the miracle. How in this isolated place are we ever going to be able to fulfill the *mitzvah* of *pirsumei nissa?* We can put the candles at the right height; we can light them before supper, at the right time; but who will see them? The birds?"

At first, his father sat quietly. Finally he sighed. "You know, Avi, that I go where I am sent and I haven't much to say about it. I succeeded in getting the assignment in Denver and you certainly had a good four years there. Of course it's hard for you now. Still, this assignment is only for a short time, and the money I make here will pay for your stay at *Yeshivah* High School dormitory in a few years.

"Since you do love Hawaii, I thought it would make up for things a bit," he continued. "You really didn't mind till now ... It's just this *Chanukah* thing, hmmmm?" Mr. Gross mused aloud. "Well, Avi, let me teach you something. *Hashem* does not want us to worry about what we cannot help in these things. You must do that part of the *mitzvah* that is in your hands. You must prepare and light the *menorah* and recite the *brachos* over it; as for the rest, just have faith that *Hashem* will do His part, too. Even if in the end there would be no one else to see the candles and *pirsumei nissa* is limited to the minimum — just our family — we would still have done our part."

Avi was not that easily consoled. Somehow all the vague dissatisfactions he had felt with his life here now assumed greater importance. The rapidly approaching *Chanukah* made him wonder about some of the other holidays. What would happen on *Purim?* His father had a *Megillah* but what about *shalach manos* (gifts to friends) and *matanos la'evyonim* (gifts to the poor)? To whom will they be given?

The next day, Mrs. Gross tried her hand at comforting Avi: "Don't take it so hard. There are almost two more weeks until *Chanukah.* Perhaps we will get some company by then. Mr. Wolfe from the Parks Department is due to come out soon and maybe some tourists will come by."

Mr. Wolfe isn't really expected for a month, Avi thought to himself, and tourists usually pass by in the daytime and go home before evening. Yet he said nothing aloud because he saw that his mother was trying to make him feel better; why should she know that she was not succeeding? But Mrs. Gross knew.

The time of *Chanukah* came close. Instead of the snow that the Grosses remembered from other years, there were blue skies and brilliant sunsets. In the kitchen a special table was set up near the window facing the highway, and Avi, who had learned that oil was better to use than candles, was rolling cotton into long thin wicks. For the remainder of the week the family had been unusually subdued, for they were all aware of how much it would mean to Avi to be able to fulfill the *mitzvah* of *pirsumei nissa,* how it would make *Chanukah* more meaningful. It seemed as though there was no hope. In the meantime, as Avi's father had said, they all did their part.

It was an hour before candle lighting time and Mrs. Gross was bustling about in the kitchen when Mr. Gross burst through the door with unaccustomed speed. The worry lines on his forehead were momentarily eased as the delicious smell of Mrs. Gross' frying *latkes* wafted out the kitchen door to him, but they quickly deepened again.

"There's a storm coming," he said, pointing out the window. Sure enough, as Avi turned, he saw the sky rapidly blackening. Without much talk, the Grosses stopped what they were doing to close storm windows and lock doors. It seemed only moments until the storm hit.

In the excitement no one paid much attention to Avi, but then, as the rain pounded against the windows, and they caught their breaths, they noticed Avi staring forlornly out the window at the gray blackness. They knew what he was thinking. Now the last hope, dim as it had been, was gone. Now, surely, no one could possibly come. Not even one person.

"Come, Avi," said Mr. Gross. "It's time to *daven Maariv* and then to light the *Chanukah* lights. We'll light them, and play *dreidel,* and you'll feel better. After all, *Chanukah* is a happy *Yom Tov* when *Hashem* performed a great miracle. We can't keep our lights waiting, just as *Hashem* didn't keep the Jews waiting for the oil."

Mr. Gross and Avi each lit his own *menorah* near the kitchen window, and then went to the living room for a *dreidel* game. As the game got more exciting and the lights flickered from the next

room, the happiness of *Chanukah* did make Avi feel a little better.

Suddenly there was a loud banging from outside. Mr. Gross jumped up and ran to the door. As he opened it, three drenched figures stumbled in and stood in the hall in the middle of three rapidly growing puddles.

All talked at once. It seemed that a bus loaded with tourists from the mainland became stranded with a flat tire on the way to Hilo. Two passengers and the driver, without raincoats and with only one flashlight, had volunteered to find the ranger station that the bus driver knew was nearby.

"We'd never have found it," said the driver, "if not for those flames! It really was a miracle that you happened to have them lit."

So it was that the Grosses had a whole busload of company for *pirsumei nissa* on the first night of *Chanukah* … While Mr. Gross went to get them in his pickup truck, Mrs. Gross made more *latkes*. After they arrived and ate, Avi started to explain to them about *Chanukah*.

One man, who introduced himself as Mr. Brenner from Chicago, started to smile.

"You needn't bother explaining, son," he said. "I and four others have *menoros* set up in our hotel room in Hilo, waiting for us."

Mr. Gross and Avi quickly arranged to lend these guests candles and candlesticks to perform the *mitzvah* on their own.

Soon afterwards, Miriam had everyone playing *dreidel*. All in all, it was a most satisfactory evening.

The next day, after the guests left, overjoyed Avi calmed down enough to talk about what had happened. *"Hashem* really made two miracles with our one light," he said to his father. "He made a *nes* (miracle) for the bus passengers when our light showed them how to find us, but he also made a *nes* for us, and we fulfilled the *mitzvah* of *pirsumei nissa* in its finest form."

"Perhaps," replied Mr. Gross, "we may not have to depend on such miracles next year. I wrote to the Department of Interior that I must be near a large city because I can't handle your education anymore. Today, I got a letter saying they are considering it. Who knows? Maybe next year we'll be near Denver again."

Flames in the Night

by Rabbi Zevulun Weisberger

"Where have you been, Yehudah?" Mrs. Greenfield asked her son. "You are late for supper again!"

"Over at a friend's house, Mom," the tall boy answered. "I was ... helping him with some homework."

"A friend? Who is it?"

"Oh, you really don't know him. His name is Sammy Hirsch and he lives on Whitehall Street."

"Sammy Hirsch? I never heard his name mentioned before. Is he a new one?"

"Well, I've known him for a short while."

This was the first conversation regarding Sammy Hirsch, but certainly not the last. After supper, the Greenfield family took the *menoros* down from the closet to clean and polish for the coming *Chanukah* holiday. Shoshanah, Yehudah's sister, handed him his *menorah.*

"Here's yours, Yehudah. It needs a lot of cleaning before it will be ready."

Yehudah took it, cleaned it in a matter-of-fact way, and quickly returned it to the closet. His mind seemed elsewhere. To the family this was strange, for he was always the most particular one about his *menorah.* He would usually spend hours polishing it and fussing over it until it was perfect.

His behavior was unusual in other ways too. Yehudah spent long hours away from home after *yeshivah* classes were over and he was constantly coming home late for supper. When he even skipped a football game with his friends, the Greenfields knew "something was up" and questions started to be asked. It was always his new friend, Sammy. They were doing some "homework" together. They had some "important things" to take care of. What was it? Yehudah never answered those questions clearly. There was an aura of mystery around it.

Even Mr. Greenfield got into the picture one evening when Yehudah came late again. "How's Sammy today?" he asked his son.

"Oh, he's all right," Yehudah answered casually.

"What's this top-secret project you two are working on?" Mr. Greenfield smiled.

"Well, it's not really classified information," Yehudah replied, also smiling. "Let's talk about more important things, like *Chanukah*. Is there anything we need for the holiday — a new *menorah* perhaps, some oil or wicks?"

"No," Mr. Greenfield answered. "So it's too confidential to discuss? Tell me, is Sammy a government agent or someone on a hush-hush mission?"

"Oh, Dad," Yehudah exclaimed, "Can't someone have a friend anymore, without everyone imagining all sorts of things?"

* * *

It was the day before *Chanukah*. The Greenfield family prepared the *menoros* near the window early. They were polished, the oil was ready, and the tray was placed underneath.

Mr. Greenfield always managed to get back from work a little earlier during *Chanukah* so he could be with the family for *hadlakas haneiros* (lighting of the candles). The children were dismissed from school earlier than usual so that they could be home early to kindle the *menorah*. Only Yehudah was absent. As he left for the *yeshivah* in the morning, he said, "Oh, by the way, don't wait for me for the *hadlakah* (lighting). I'll be a little late."

"You mean you are not going to be with us! Where will you be?" Shoshanah asked him.

"At Sammy's. I'll light it there." With these words, he turned and left the house.

The family exchanged glances. "Oh boy — something must really be going on if Yehudah would miss *hadlakas haneiros* with his family for this friend of his — what could it possibly be?" his brother, Naftali, said.

"I don't know — I don't know. But if this continues much longer, we'll have to get to the bottom of this. I'm losing patience with this new friendship of his," remarked his mother. She decided to call Sammy's house, with a request that Yehudah should leave early. Alas — she had neither his address nor his number.

True to his word, Yehudah was not present at the kindling of the first *Chanukah* flame. Mr. Greenfield was very irritated. "It's not easy for me to leave my business early each night of *Chanukah*. If I can be here in time, then Yehudah can be here in time. This Sammy business has gone much too far. Tonight we'll solve this mystery once and for all!"

In a short while, Yehudah arrived home. He seemed to be

very happy. He smiled as he entered and declared, "Happy *Chanukah* to all."

"Where did you light the candles, Yehudah?" his father asked."

"At Sammy's house."

"Why didn't you come home to join us? In our family, we light together. Once and for all, I want to know what is so important in Sammy's house that you have to be there whenever you're supposed to be here."

"Please, Dad, I know it seems queer. Just trust me for a few more days and then, I promise, I'll explain everything. You'll be proud, Dad, just give me a little time. I never let you down."

Mr. and Mrs. Greenfield looked at each other. They liked the affair less and less, but Yehudah was so sincere that they had to give in and agree to wait.

Thus ended the conversation at the supper table, but not the speculation. After supper, Shoshanah and Naftali got together and made a whispered decision to play detective and solve the mystery. Naftali was to follow Yehudah home from school to Sammy's house. Somehow he would find an excuse to enter the house, and then he would know. Naftali traded coats and hats with a friend so that he could get onto Yehudah's bus without being recognized.

"Operation Follow" was executed the next day. He noticed that Yehudah took the Crosstown bus to the West Side of town. He got off the bus and walked down the block to a modest looking house. Yehudah entered while Naftali stood watching from a doorway across the street. Soon it was dark. Naftali

noticed figures at one of the side windows. There were a few people there including Yehudah. After the candles were lit, Naftali knocked at the door. Imagine the surprise on his brother's face when he saw him!

"How did you find this place, Naftali?" Yehudah asked, "And what do you want?"

Before Naftali answered, he looked around the room. There were a man and a woman and a young boy. The boy was standing near his *menorah* admiring the beauty of the candles. There was a happy look on his face. Yehudah got over his surprise and recovered his manners.

"This is Sammy Hirsch, Naftali," Yehudah said, smiling.

"Your secret friend? He's so young!" Naftali exclaimed.

"Yes, he's Sammy, my friend," Yehudah said, holding his arm around him. "Oh, well, I guess I should go home now. You'll be able to take care of the candlelighting yourself now, Sammy. You are an expert already!''

Mr. Hirsch now approached Yehudah and shook his hand. "We are very grateful for your help. I must admit we're impressed, and we're going to consider your suggestion very seriously."

"Oh, fine, Mr. Hirsch. It would be the best thing you ever did for Sammy. You will never regret it," Yehudah replied beaming.

With a cheery "Happy *Chanukah,*" the brothers left. "Now the whole story will be told, Sherlock Holmes. You must have

been following me!" Yehudah complained to Naftali.

At the supper table, the mystery of "friend Sammy" was finally cleared up. Sammy was going to public school, and Yehudah met him at a Release Hour program. The boy was impressed by the discussion of the forthcoming holiday, but told Yehudah sadly that he was unable to make the *brachos* and, therefore, felt he couldn't kindle the *menorah*. He didn't go to any *yeshivah* or Hebrew school. He felt quite sad about it.

Yehudah had tried to convince Sammy's parents to send him to a *yeshivah*, but to no avail. In his many visits to the Hirsch home, he started to teach Sammy the *brachos* with a crash course in *aleph-beis.* The first night of *Chanukah,* as Sammy kindled the *menorah* and sang the *brachos* with the proper tune, Yehudah stood alongside him. He noticed the joy in Sammy's face and all the efforts of the past few months seemed worthwhile. Even more hopeful were the looks on his parents' faces and their interest. After the second night, Yehudah let Sammy handle it on his own. Even better, Mr. and Mrs. Hirsch seemed to be ready to enroll Sammy in the *yeshivah*.

Mr. Greenfield was silent for a while after listening to the story. "Well, Yehudah, while we were all kindling the *menorah* with ordinary wicks, you were also lighting a flame. But yours will burn for a longer time — a flame inside a Jewish boy. Another Yehudah, in the days of the *Beis Hamikdash,* once did the same thing."

"Now that the secret is out, Yehudah," said his mother, "why don't you invite Mr. Mystery Friend over with his parents. We'd love to meet them."

A Modern Day Chanukah Victory

by Rena (Brown) Kaplan

A few hours ago I had been standing in front of the room teaching my tenth grade mathematics students. Now I was huddled in a corner of the coat closet hoping no one would come in and find me. I was waiting for the custodian to finish his last cleaning chores somewhere in the three story school building. Then he would pull the main electrical switch and plunge the building into darkness. When that happened I would be all alone this Friday night — and safe. At least I would be safe until school re-opened on Monday morning.

The moment came. The lights were out. I waited a few minutes, then left my hiding place in the coat closet, stretched my legs, stumbled in the dark as I tried to find my desk, and sat down. It might be my last time sitting in this chair; at least I would have a long, undisturbed night to spend in it.

I thought of my children a few miles away. They were probably asking my husband, "Where is Mommy? Why didn't she come home for *Shabbos?*"

And my husband was saying, "Mommy had to go away to friends this *Shabbos.*"

"Who are these friends? Mommy never goes away for a *Shabbos.* How are we supposed to have a real Jewish *Shabbos* if Mommy isn't here?"

Living as Orthodox Jews in Kishinev, Russia in the 1960's is hardly pleasant. Keeping a Jewish *Shabbos* is a crime as far as the government is concerned. Yet in our home, the *Shabbos* remains the highlight of the week. On this day we use the china, have something delicious on the menu, and, most important, we relive part of our heritage. The children know *Shabbos* is forbidden, but they wait for *Shabbos* anxiously. The *Shabbos* meals are the highlight of the week and they wait for it all through the six days. They are surprised and probably angry that I am not there to share it with them. How I wish I were there!

As I sat in the dark, I thought back to the events of the day that led up to my *Shabbos* in the dark.

A year ago I was working as a graduate electrical engineer. Although I liked the work, I knew that I would be required to work on *Shabbos*. Therefore I decided to resign. I snatched at a chance to become a teacher, thinking that it would be easier for me to observe the *Shabbos*. The schools were open on *Shabbos*, but each teacher was allowed one day off a week. I asked my supervisor to assign Saturday as my free day. She suspected me of being a religious Jew and she began spying on me. I was always on guard when she was around and I tried to keep from letting her learn anything about my private life.

Teachers were required to write daily reports of each student's progress. Every day after dismissal, the supervisor herself would give us the forms to fill out. Before we would leave the building we would leave the completed reports on the supervisor's desk in her office. The first thing she did each day was to inspect all the logs. Knowing that she watched my every move looking for ways to cause me trouble, I was always very careful in doing my classroom report. Although I was disturbed by the supervisor's attitude and obvious spying on me, I was grateful that there had never been any open argument with her.

That was until today.

An official government holiday had been declared for the weekend, so the Friday schedule was changed. My assignment sheet required me to conduct a late 3:00 P.M. class on this day. In these winter months *Shabbos* begins early. I was always in a mad rush to finish my report and get home in time for *Shabbos* during wintertime. Often I would walk all the way home to avoid riding on *Shabbos*. But today, with my late class, it would already be *Shabbos* by the time class was dismissed! When would I fill in my report?

If I did it right after class I would be desecrating the *Shabbos*. If I left it for after *Shabbos*, the supervisor would notice on Monday morning that it was missing. She would have me fired and almost certainly get me arrested and put on trial as disloyal to the state. My husband and I discussed the problem and agreed that we had to try a very risky plan.

After I received my forms at dismissal, I returned to my classroom. And there I remained even as I began to hear sounds of the other teachers leaving. Wary of being seen, I peered cautiously out the window, enviously watching the other teachers leave the school building.

Gradually the building became silent until the only sound I could hear was the ceaseless moaning of the winter wind against the windows. Then ... a noise ... a thud ... I leaped breathlessly into the coat closet. *Have I been discovered?* My heartbeat pounded louder than the wind outside. I held my breath. Then I recognized the noise. I stole a quick glance out of the closet — yes, I was right. The custodian was mopping up the floor. It took about two hours more for him to complete all the classrooms. Then … the electricity went off. I waited alone in the dark and cold, in that noiseless, deserted building.

I spent that entire *Shabbos,* night and day, in the school. As soon as it became dark, I filled in my report by candlelight. Then with candle clutched in one hand and the report in the other, I tiptoed cautiously down the corridor toward the supervisor's office. Barely able to see a few feet ahead of me by the flickering candlelight, I was struck by the strange, frightening appearance of the same hallway which I had casually passed through so many times every day. Without the noisy crowds of jostling students, the corridor was drab, colorless, and eerie.

Finally, I reached the door of the supervisor's office. At last! Even though the building was deserted, I turned the handle very slowly, very carefully, so that it wouldn't creak. *The door wouldn't budge.* I tried again in vain. The door was locked. How was I to get my report onto my supervisor's desk, before she herself opened the door on Monday morning?

I was emotionally drained. The tensions of the past twenty-four hours — or was it the past year, or possibly an entire life as a religious Jew — overcame me. I thought of the terrible fate that awaited me on Monday morning when the supervisor discovered that my report wasn't there. She surely knew that the report wouldn't be there. My attempt to outwit her had failed. By making the attempt I had lost a chance to spend my last *Shabbos* with my family. Tomorrow night was *Chanukah.* And I would probably spend it in prison!

Chanukah … holiday of light and inspiration … Maccabees against Syrians — outnumbered but not defeated … strength of faith versus strength of arms … We won … I thought of Antiochus … I thought of my supervisor … I thought, *"I'll find a way out."*

I glanced frantically up and down the hall, searching for a clue, an idea, anything to get that door open. Several rooms away I noticed the custodian's utility closet. The door was open. Breathing heavily I ran toward the closet. I don't know what I expected to find. But there, hanging from a rusted nail amid an array of pails, brushes, and tools was a key ring. There were not less than thirty keys of various sizes and shapes dangling from it. I grabbed the bunch of keys and frantically began trying each one in the door. I shuddered. Who knew if the custodian might appear unexpectedly? My hands were shaking and sweating and I couldn't keep the keys from jingling and rattling as I unsuccessfully went through most of them. I slipped the next one into the key hole. *I turned!* נֵס גָּדוֹל הָיָ' פֹּה! A great miracle happened *here!* The door swung open. I dashed in, and stood still a moment to gain full control of myself. I carefully placed my report in the middle of the pile. Locking the door behind me, I carefully slipped out of the building through a side door and went home — my Jewish home — to my brave husband, and our children.

The next night I stood in front of the first *Chanukah* light and watched its story unfold as the flame danced about the wick. Then I lingered. The *Chanukah* story wasn't over. This year we had, with *Hashem's* help, written another chapter to the ancient story of *Chanukah.*

Chanukah on the Golan

by Yaffa Ganz

It is during the period when the Syrians were shooting into Israeli settlements and army positions on the Golan Heights in the north of Israel, and Arab terrorists were constantly trying to infiltrate across the border to bomb or kidnap. The Israeli army is in a high state of alert and the borders are carefully watched. Yossi, Nissim, and Shabtai are in the border patrol.

"Hey! It's my birthday tonight!"

"*Mazel Tov!* It's also the first night of *Chanukah*, but we won't have much of a celebration up here in our bunker."

Yossi, Nissim, and Shabtai were each sitting behind artillery and machine guns sticking out of little openings in a bunker up on the Golan in the north of Israel. The section of the Golan they were on was overlooking the city of Teveriah. The guns, of course, were pointed not towards Teveriah, but to the northeast — towards Syria.

"I *know* it's the first night of *Chanukah*," said Nissim. "Why do you think I was called *Nissim* (Miracles)? And why can't we celebrate up here? I don't need a birthday party; even if no one makes me a party, I still get to light *Chanukah* candles!"

"Yeh, but the celebration is for *Chanukah* and not for you!" said Shabtai, laughing.

"Why can't I feel that it's for me too? After all, how many people are there in the world who were born on the first night of *Chanukah* and named Nissim? Besides, remembering the original *Chanukah* makes me feel a lot better about risking my life up here; it makes me think of the old story of the few fighting against the many; of people not wanting to leave *Am Yisrael* (the Jewish Nation) alone; of our enemies wanting to destroy us in our own land. And just as the *Maccabim* put their trust in *Hashem* and went out to fight the enemies of *Am Yisrael,* we're doing the same thing!"

"Well, I have sad news for you," said Yossi. "This year you won't do *any* celebrating, personal or not. We have no candles."

"But we have rifle oil. And there's enough to burn for half an hour at least. You don't think I'd forget *Chanukah,* especially when it's my birthday, do you?"

"Since when can you use rifle oil for *Chanukah?*" asked Yossi. "Everybody always lights with olive oil or candles!"

"Because all oil is kosher for *Chanukah* lighting," said Nissim triumphantly.

"Well, we have no *menorah.*"

"Wrong again. Here are eight empty bullet cases and one larger one for a *shamash.* They aren't very elegant, but under the circumstances, they will do. And I can use cotton from the first aid kit for wicks. I'll put them on a piece of wood in a straight line. Be prepared! That's my motto!"

"You're insane!" said Shabtai, getting angry. "Where do you think you're going to light candles? This bunker is so small and crowded that if you don't burn us to death you'll suffocate us with smoke."

"Let me think," said Yossi. "We were ordered not to light cigarettes or flashlights of any kind, but no one said anything about *Chanukah* candles."

"Very funny," answered Shabtai. "I guarantee you that Yehudah *Hamaccabee* wouldn't have lit candles or done anything else to endanger his men when they were fighting."

"That depends on what you consider dangerous," said Nissim. "How much do you know about Yehudah *Hamaccabee* anyway? *Everything* he did seemed too dangerous to some people. He was fighting against the tremendous Syrian army. He started out with no equipment, few arms, no organization, no nothing! Just a minute. I take that back. He did have something very important. He had *emunah* (belief) in *Hashem*. He knew that the Jews were fighting to keep *Eretz Yisrael* safe for Jews and for the Torah. He knew that if *Eretz Yisrael* stopped being a place where Jews could learn Torah and keep *mitzvos,* then they would *really* be in trouble."

"Maybe," mumbled Shabtai. "But he certainly didn't do things like lighting candles and giving away his position to the enemy! Besides, what about that band of terrorists that's loose in these hills? Our patrols spotted them, but they got away each time. Three Arabs with grenades and machine guns — do you want to light up our positions to give them a target? You'll get a grenade and a *full* bullet case as a birthday present."

"But we won't just be lighting candles for a birthday," countered Yossi. "We'll be doing a *mitzvah* — and that's sure worth a risk."

"Did you ever read what kind of unmilitary things Yehudah *Hamaccabee* did when they went out to fight?" asked Nissim. "They had the whole army *daven* (pray) three times a day, and before they went out to each battle, they all said a special *tefillah* (prayer) asking *Hashem* to help them. And at first, they wouldn't even fight on *Shabbos.* Only after the Syrians purposely kept attacking on *Shabbos* did they fight on *Shabbos* too, because it was *pikuach nefesh* (necessary to save a life). I don't think Yehudah *Hamaccabee* would have thought that observing a *mitzvah* in the middle of a war is silly!"

"I'll tell you the truth," said Yossi, "if I had known we would be sent up here for *Chanukah,* I would have asked a rabbi where or how we should light the candles. Lighting candles could be endangering our lives. It makes a first class target!"

"I have good news for you," said Nissim. "I *did* ask the Rabbi of our unit. The law is that if lighting the candles is dangerous because the enemy can see them, then you light them in a hidden or sheltered place. So I have an idea. We won't light them inside the bunker; I'd hate to suffocate poor Shabtai! But there's this huge boulder right outside the bunker and if we light on our side of the rock, then *we'll* be able to see it but the Syrians won't!"

"I still don't like the idea," said Shabtai. "What about those three terrorists? For all we know they may be right on top of us this minute."

"Well, it's better than lighting it in here, and I *am* going to light it somewhere!" said Nissim.

So Nissim took his empty bullet cases and the pieces of cotton for wicks, some matches and his rifle oil, and prepared to crawl out of the bunker to the rock.

Just then, Nissim got the birthday present they all dreaded. There was a splatter of bullets over their heads. A grenade flew over the bunker and exploded against the rock Nissim had just pointed out. An arm reached into the bunker and tossed a grenade inside. It landed on the ground and Shabtai dove on top of it so that the explosion would kill only him and not all three.

Yossi grabbed at the outstretched arm, pulling and twisting it with all his might, and — as the terrorist's head came into view — Nissim shot. Yossi and Nissim dashed to their gun positions and saw the other two terrorists scrambling across the rocky hill. Two quick machine gun bursts, and the terrorist menace was removed from that area of the Golan.

Limp with emotion, Yossi and Nissim turned around to look at Shabtai. He was still flat on the ground, but a look of disbelief was on his face. Slowly, carefully, he stood up. There, where his stomach had been just seconds earlier, was a Russian grenade. Shabtai waved his comrades away, saying, "Let me take care of it. I should have been dead by now, anyway."

Very gently, he picked it up and hurled it out of the bunker. It clattered down the hillside harmlessly and then — it exploded. Slowly, Shabtai turned and faced his friends. After a moment they rushed to him and embraced him. He had been ready to give his life to save theirs — but *Hashem* wanted them all to live.

"It was a modern *Chanukah* miracle!" cried Shabtai. "Nissim, you are right. We will *all* kindle the *Chanukah* lights and *Hashem* will protect us as He protected the *Maccabees.*"

"Shabtai, look!" called Yossi. He pointed to Nissim's rock. The first grenade had blasted a hole in it, forming a shelf — a perfect shelf in the rock — just the right size for their homemade *Chanukah* lights!

After they lit and sang *Hanerot Halalu* and *Ma'oz Tzur* they looked down the mountain to Teveriah. There were hundreds of tiny lights down below them. For miles around, twinkling from all the houses in Teveriah, there were little sparkling dots of light in windows and doorways, on roofs of houses and synagogues.

Yossi whistled. "We had to light our candles so they wouldn't be seen. But because we're sitting up here and guarding the people down there, they are safe to light their candles in the open. We help watch them and they help keep

Torah alive for us."

"And as I told you," continued Nissim, "I never missed a birthday celebration yet! Even if no one makes me a party, I always have *Chanukah!*"

The Book of Remedies

A story from the Midrash

retold by Rabbi Elchonon (Charles) Wengrov

It was many, many years ago that a man and his wife lived together in great unhappiness — for they were childless. They were getting old, and it seemed as though they would never have a child. And so, though they were very rich, they spent their days in sorrow. Every day the rich man would go to the *yeshivah* to stand by the window and listen to the children learning. Tears would roll down his cheeks, and he would say to himself, "Of what use is my wealth to me if I have no son to learn *Hashem's* holy Torah?"

One day, in a moment of despair, he took all his money and gave it away to the men who sat all day in the *beis midrash* and studied the Torah. Without a son, he felt he had no use for the money. But strange! Exactly a year after he gave his money away his wife bore him a son.

How happy they were now, the man and his wife. They waited eagerly for the child to grow up, and when the boy was five, his father proudly walked with him to the nearest *yeshivah*. The *rebbi* was glad to receive the new pupil, but the boy's father would not let him sit down right away in the class.

"Tell me first," said the proud father, "what will this class learn this coming year?"

"Our children begin with *Vayikra*, the third book of

Chumash," replied the *rebbi.*

"Please help me," said the old man. "I want my little boy to be taught *Bereishis* also. I want him to learn the great, wonderful story of how *Hashem* created the world and chose Avraham and his children to serve Him. Since I gave away all my money, I cannot hire someone to teach my son privately. Will you teach him *Bereishis?* Please?"

The *rebbi* agreed, and the boy began to go to *yeshivah.* And though the father was old, he took his son on the long walk to and from the school every day. For, after all, was not the little boy his pride and joy? But the boy was a bright lad, and he soon noticed that it made his father very tired to go all the way from the house to the school and from the school to the house. At the end of each trip his father would be breathing hard, and he would have to sit down, completely exhausted. One day the boy said to his father, "Please let me go to *yeshivah* by myself. The distance is very tiring for you. And, besides, I know the way myself. I promise you I'll be careful."

So from that day on the boy went by himself, the beloved book of *Bereishis* in his hand. He was happy, for he liked to learn the story of the creation of the world. But even happier was his father, for at last his greatest wish had come true. He had a son of his own who was learning well at the *yeshivah*.

One morning, the boy was on his way to school, happily watching the birds twittering in the trees. His heart was light, and he barely heard the coach that was coming up behind him. In the coach sat a duke, a close friend of the king of the land. The duke leaned out the coach window, and saw a bright, fair-haired boy walking happily along. The nobleman decided it would be fun to take the child to his home and bring him up as a royal pageboy. The duke gave an order to his driver, and almost instantly he stopped the coach, seized the boy, and rode off with the struggling lad crying in the back.

The hours of the day passed. It was time at last for their beloved son to come home from school. His parents waited for him — but he did not come home. Worried and anxious, the father went to the *yeshivah*. On the way he asked every person that he met, "Have you seen a little boy walking along this way?

He is about so high, with fair hair, and he wore a blue coat … You're sure you didn't see him?" So he went along, peering anxiously in every direction, but in vain. No sign of his dear son did he see, and when he found that everyone had gone home from the *yeshivah* he was terribly frightened. He ran to the *rebbi's* home — and was told that his son had not been in *yeshivah* that day! He went home, and, with a breaking heart, told his wife the news. Together they cried and mourned for their vanished son. Would they ever see him again? From that time on, they were always sorrowful and no one could comfort them. Their only child was gone.

The duke who had kidnapped the child lived in the king's palace. Here he brought his captive to grow up as a pageboy. But the child paid no attention to what the palace servants tried to teach him. He knew that he did not belong here. He belonged with his parents, and he wanted to go to them. Meanwhile, he had his book of *Bereishis* with him, and as often as he could, he read through the beautiful sentences that he had learned. He was afraid that the duke would take the holy book away from him because he was not learning to be a good pageboy. One day he found the palace library, the room where all the king's books were kept, and he carefully put his book of *Bereishis* on a shelf near the bottom. He was sure no one would notice it there. And as for himself, whenever he wanted to learn he could sneak in there and take it out.

Soon after this, the king was stricken with a strange illness. The royal physicians could find nothing wrong with him. He seemed perfectly healthy, yet he was restless. He could neither sleep nor eat. He couldn't even sit still. A strange nervousness possessed him.

One night he grew angry at his physicians and shouted at them, "All right, you fools, bring the *Book of Remedies.* There you will find a remedy for every kind of disease. If you can't cure me even after you read through the *Book of Remedies,* I'll have your heads! Do you hear?"

One of them rushed at once to the library to find the *Book of Remedies.* He bent down to take it from the shelf next to the bottom. In his great fright he didn't see that the book was not the *Book of Remedies* at all, but *Bereishis,* the first book of the Torah.

The king seized the book and opened it. He turned the pages eagerly. "Let's see now," he said, "where would I find the disease of restlessness?" And then he looked up slowly. He glowered angrily at the physician, who trembled with fear before him. "What fool trick is this?" he bellowed. "Since when is the *Book of Remedies* written in a strange, undecipherable language? Quickly, read it to me or I'll have your heads."

The terrified physicians took the book with shaking hands. Not one of them could read a single letter of it. There was a moment of silence. Then a meek voice spoke up, "I believe this is … er … Hebrew, your Majesty. It is possible that there is someone in the building … er … a small boy … who may be able to read this. I … er … shall inquire." With that, the one who spoke went to get the boy from the duke's room.

The lad was brought. He stood before the king in great fear, for he didn't know why he was called. He thought he would be punished for not being a good page. But when he saw his beloved book of *Bereishis,* he smiled. And when he was told to read it, he quickly opened it at the beginning and began reading the story of the Creation. He explained every sentence carefully, slowly. And as the king listened, a strange thing happened. He became calm. The restlessness left him, and he felt well again! And all from listening to the story of the Creation, how *Hashem* had made heaven and earth and all that lived in them.

The king smiled contentedly. "My boy," he said, "that is

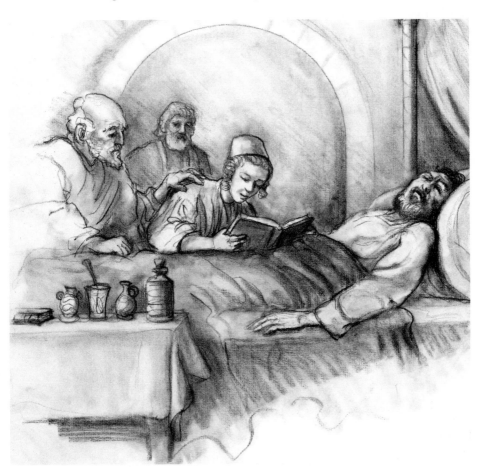

really a wonderful book of remedies you have there. You have just made me well. Ask for anything you want, and I'll give it to you."

For a moment the boy couldn't speak. Then he took courage, and in a small voice he asked, "Please, Your Highness, may I go home?"

An hour later, a royal coach came to a stop before the house of his parents, and the little boy jumped out. He ran inside, and right into the arms of his mother and father. For a long time all three cried with joy — and they hardly saw the palace servants who brought in bags of gold from the coach, a small present from the king.

The Precious Gift

by Rabbi Zevulun Weisberger

I t was dark in the room. It really should not have been so, for it was only 3:00 P.M., and it was a bright, sunny day. Elchanan Rosen was just waking up from a deep sleep. Things were not as clear as they should have been, and this troubled Elchanan. In fact, he seemed to be having difficulty recognizing things …

"Why can't I see straight?" he asked, alarmed.

"You are lucky you can see at all, Elchanan," answered a nurse who was hovering over his bed in the Pleasantville Hospital. "That was quite a serious accident you were in, you know."

"Accident? Oh, yes. I remember it now. That was some mess in Mr. Benson's brand new car!"

"Don't strain yourself too much, Elchanan," the nurse said. "The doctor will correct things. But you must save your strength in case you need an operation."

"An operation! Would it be a serious one?" the young boy asked.

"Well, anything dealing with the eyes is serious. But Dr. Green is an expert. If anything can be done, I'm sure he's the one to do it."

Elchanan became uneasy. Eyesight is one of the most important faculties a person has. Without it, one is lost … How had he ever gotten into such a predicament?

He started to recall the day of the accident. It had started like an ordinary Sunday. He had gone to bed early the previous evening determined to get up for the *minyan* on time. After awakening the next morning, there had been a short battle with his *yeitzer harah* (evil inclination), but Elchanan won and he was soon up and out of bed. Quickly he washed and dressed, dashed down the stairs, and arrived in *shul* before you could count "ten." The *minyan* was just starting and the rush was on. Elchanan opened his *siddur* and hurried through *Mah Tovu* and the *Bircas Hatorah*. The *Bircas Hashachar* went particularly fast. Elchanan was always proud of his record of reciting all of the *brachos* in less than sixty seconds. This speed came in handy at times as when he arrived late to *minyan,* but was also helpful on other occasions as well.

His *chaver* (friend), Yoseif, on the other hand, objected to his speed. *"Davening* is no race," he would say. "We are *davening* to *Hashem,* not just mumbling words. If you would only think how these words in the *siddur* are *your* words spoken to *Hashem,* you wouldn't be such a speed-demon at *Shacharis* and you'd try to concentrate on some of your *davening!"*

Elchanan would often recall Yoseif's words as he was zooming through the *tefillos,* but he had repeated the prayers so often that it was hard to concentrate. After breakfast, he went to the *yeshivah* for the morning session. It was an unseasonably warm day, and he decided to join his friends at the ball field during the afternoon. Shimmy Benson's father had offered to give him a ride in his new car. Elchanan recalled that it had started to rain. There was a heavy downpour. The car rounded a curve, and then — BANG! — the collision with the green sedan that skidded into their path. That was all he remembered. Now he had awakened with a horrible throbbing in his head, and the vagueness in his eyes.

"You've been here three days already, son," the nurse remarked. "The accident happened Sunday afternoon, and it's Wednesday now."

"Three days! You mean I have been out for three days? Wow! It seems like it just happened."

Elchanan was worried. What would happen if the operation were not successful? How would he get around? He thought of Mr. Lampkin, the blinded veteran of World War II, who lived down the block. A huge dog on a leash led him through traffic, and somehow he managed his business as a bookstore proprietor ... But how would he, Elchanan, manage? Learning,

davening, playing baseball — a seeing-eye dog could never help him do these things. At times he imagined coming to class with a dog on a leash, but the fun of seeing the boys' reaction and the *rebbi's* wouldn't be his! Instead, the agony of fumbling was most immediate in his mind. He was in a deep state of gloom when his parents came to visit him.

"Don't worry, Elchanan," Mr. Rosen said. "It is in *Hashem's* hands. He grants us the gift of eyesight. He is the *Pokayach Ivrim* — the One Who gives vision — a blessing we enjoy every day, and mention each morning. He will surely help you now, too.

Pokayach Ivrim — A *brachah* Elchanan had uttered so many times. Never before had he realized its significance — the depth of *Hashem's* gift to mankind. He had always taken it for granted and never really expressed gratitude for this invaluable gift. And now it might never be his again.

* * *

Dr. Green decided to operate on the very next day. After a few hours it was over, and Elchanan was wheeled back to his room, his eyes covered with bandages.

The pain was a constant companion to Elchanan, but this did not really upset him. Sooner or later it would be gone. However two gnawing questions troubled him ... Was the operation successful? Will I be able to see again, or not? The nurse gave him pills regularly to ease the pain, but those haunting questions never left him for a moment.

Finally, after a weekend that seemed endless, the bandages were removed. He opened his eyes slowly. At first everything was blurred, but soon things became a little clearer. The shades were drawn, but he could make out Dr. Green at his bedside, smiling.

"The operation was successful, Elchanan," he said. "You will have your eyesight fully restored."

Elchanan was soon smiling broadly. "Everything looks so wonderful. The sunlight is so warm and beautiful. Even the bare trees outside look magnificent."

Hashem's universe seemed to smile at him. The trees seemed to wave to him in the soft wind, and the skies seemed clearer than ever before. מַה גָּדְלוּ מַעֲשֶׂיךָ ה'!, "How great are Your works, *Hashem!*"

He picked up his *siddur*. The words seemed to shine on the white pages. He started to *daven Shacharis* with his usual speed. Suddenly, he halted. He was about to recite the *brachah Pokayach Ivrim*. But no — he could not recite this *brachah* as usual. This was something special. His eyesight had been restored by the kindness of *Hashem*. One must be grateful, and not take things for granted. He never uttered a *brachah* with so much *kavanah* (feeling) in his life … It was his way of saying "Thank you, *Hashem*," for a precious gift.

A Tree Afloat

by Rabbi Binyamin (Bernard) Goldenberg

It was a beautiful mansion. And you could see immediately that it was owned by a very rich man. Wherever you turned you saw bustling and hustling servants. And wherever your gaze traveled you were immediately impressed by the brilliant display of beautiful gold and silver ornaments. Yes, there was no doubt that here, in a beautiful suburb near Jerusalem, lived a man of great wealth. He was famous as a very rich man, but he was also famous as the country's best-known miser — a wretched miser who, despite his riches, never gave a piece of bread to a beggar or a night's lodging to a wanderer.

Right now this very rich man was in his office, making ready to take inventory of all his wealth. This he did only once a year and today was the day. All around him were large heavy steel safes — and smaller steel cash boxes. In the safes were diamonds and rubies. And in the steel boxes were neatly counted bundles of money, usually 5,000 *dinars* to a bundle.

As the very rich man began to look in his pocket for his key to the cash boxes he began to fell uncomfortably hot. He opened his shirt collar, but that did not help. He went over to the window and opened it. The day was calm, just a mild breeze every now and then — but just as the rich man turned around a sudden gust

of wind began to swirl around in the garden below. For a moment, the rich man turned around toward the window, and just as he did, he noticed that the unexpected gust of wind had blown a stray piece of paper through the open window. Then, just as suddenly, the wind in the garden stopped.

Annoyed, he stooped down and picked up the bit of paper to throw it in the wastebasket. And as he did so he saw that the stray bit of paper was a torn fragment of a page from *Tanach* and that it contained only one sentence from the words of the Prophet Chaggai, "Mine is the silver and mine is the gold, says *Hashem* …"

For the moment the rich man merely put the torn fragment of the *Tanach* page in his pocket, and again began to look for his key to the cash boxes. But as he approached the boxes, the entire incident began to annoy him, to disturb him, and finally to worry him. Why did he, a minute ago, feel so hot and uncomfortable when the day was so mild? What made him open that window facing the garden? Why the sudden wind? Why the stray bit of paper torn from a *Tanach?* Just what was the significance of the sentence, "Mine is the silver and mine is the gold …"?

The more he thought, the more he worried. The more he worried the less he was able to attend to his business. Somehow, at this very moment, he couldn't get himself to open the cash boxes.

He walked out of the room and with quick steps made his way to another section of the mansion to see his wife. He locked the door of her room and told her of the strange occurrence in his office with the stray bit of paper.

"What could it be? What could it be?" he kept asking over and over again.

"But look, perhaps it's nothing at all," his wife told him," just a little wind, that's all. Why worry about it?"

He refused to put his worries aside, and she, too, began to be riddled with fears. Together they kept saying over and over again, "But what could it be? What could it be?"

They felt that somehow their money was in danger, but they

didn't know why. And so, together, they devised a plan to safeguard their fortune.

Everyone was asleep and it was pitch dark outside when the rich husband and his wife sneaked out of the house. They made their way to a forest near their home. As silently as possible they drilled holes in the trunk of a tree and put all their valuables and diamonds in the holes and then filled up the holes with twigs, little branches and the like. Now they were sure that whoever had designs on their money would not be able to find it.

For the next two days the rich couple didn't budge from the forest. On the third day a violent storm arose and the couple was forced indoors. For half a day and all through the night, the storm raged. Windows were broken, trees were felled, and quite a few of the servants' shacks fell apart because of the storm's violence.

Next day, the couple hurried out to their tree in the forest. On the way, they had to clear from their path saplings and branches that the big wind had thrown down. When they reached the place in the forest, they saw, to their shock, that the place was empty and only some beat-up roots remained!

"Our tree, our tree, our wealth, our wealth," screamed the couple. "Let us do something!" said the woman. "It's possible that the wind tore out the tree and carried it to another place in the forest. Let us look."

Together they searched the forest. And although they found a few big trees felled by the storm, not one of them was their tree with the valuables.

From that day on the couple became very melancholy and sad. Things went from bad to worse. They had to send away their servants. A little while later they had to sell their mansion, and as time went on things became even worse. Before long, the two of them, dressed in tatters, had to walk through the countryside, begging kind people for a piece of bread and a night's lodging.

* * *

Two days after the storm, Avraham, a poor carpenter, was walking along a river bank near Jerusalem. Although usually in good spirits he was now rather sad and a bit bitter about his plight. For three weeks he had been out of work. There was no one left from whom he could borrow. How could he feed his family? And how would he invite *orchim* (guests) for *Shabbos?* For even though Avraham was a poor carpenter, he always made it his habit to have *orchim* at his *Shabbos* table. And now he didn't even have money for his own family.

Thus, saddened and disappointed, he walked along a river bank, not looking to his right nor to his left. Suddenly he tripped over something solid, and then fell completely on his face. "Ouch," he yelled, as he got up to brush off the sand and mud from his work clothes. As he did, he noticed that the river had washed up a storm-beaten tree onto the bank. It was on this tree that he had stumbled. Avraham muttered to himself as he continued walking when suddenly he exclaimed, "Why don't I take that tree, chop it up, and sell it in the market for firewood? At least I'll have a little money for *Shabbos!*"

Quickly, Avraham the carpenter ran back into town, brought back his mule and loaded the tree on its strong back. Once home, he took out his axe to chop up the tree for firewood. No sooner did he start than rubies, diamonds, and other valuables began to fall out of the tree. Avraham was stunned, and began to call his wife and neighbors. When he calmed down a bit he began to realize that he was now one of the richest men in Jerusalem. Overnight Avraham became famous as a very rich and charitable man. From that time on there was never a poor man in Jerusalem who had nothing to eat for *Shabbos* — for Avraham invited them all to his *Shabbos* table.

One *Erev Shabbos,* a very poor couple came to Jerusalem. They were begging from house to house. Since this was *Erev Shabbos* the couple decided to stay over in Jerusalem, especially since they had heard that there was a certain Avraham, a very rich man, who had all the poor as his *orchim* for *Shabbos* and that he treated them all as kings and nobles.

And so they found themselves on Friday night sitting at Avraham's *Shabbos* table. There they heard the whole story of Avraham's new wealth and his good heart. And there they were — they who had been so very, very rich, but who were now so very, very poor — and Avraham, once so very, very poor, but who was now so very, very rich.

When *Shabbos* was over and *Havdalah* was recited, the wife of Avraham, the carpenter, saw that these two guests were very sad. She went over to them and said, "Are you sad because *Shabbos* is over and you have to leave now? If so, you need not go. You may stay longer."

When the lady heard this she began to weep and she told Avraham's wife that she and her husband had once been very wealthy, that they had hidden their fortune in a tree, that there had been a fierce storm — and that the fortune Avraham had

found was once theirs. When Avraham's wife heard the story she called her husband and together they decided to give the money back to the once-rich couple. "Here," they said, "take all the money. It's only right. All this money is rightfully yours."

The couple looked at each other and then, with tears in her

eyes, the once-rich lady said, "No, we cannot accept it. For if the money was really destined for us then the storm and Avraham's walk along the river would never have happened. We see that the money is really intended for you — we will have none of it. We have sinned because we were never charitable, and this is our punishment."

Still, Avraham insisted. But the couple was just as insistent and refused to take the money. The only thing they did take was a cake which Avraham's wife baked for them. She didn't tell them that she had put 500 *dinars* into the cake.

A day or so later, the couple came to a bridge where they had to pay a toll. Not having any money, they begged the tollkeeper to let them through. The guard refused. Finally, the couple said, "Look, we have no money. All we have is this cake which a kindhearted person baked for us. Please take it and let us go through."

After some thought, the tollkeeper said, "Well, ordinarily you wouldn't get away with it. But it so happens that tomorrow I am going to a wedding in Jerusalem and this cake will come in handy as a wedding gift. All right then, go ahead. I'll take the cake."

The next day the tollkeeper went to the wedding in Jerusalem. He gave the beautiful cake as a gift to the groom and his parents. Everybody was happy.

Need I tell you that the groom was Avraham's son? Thus, the money in the cake came back to Avraham and his wife — for, rich or poor, they were always charitable.

A 1776 Bar Mitzvah

by Rena (Brown) Kaplan

Asher Haddad cautiously inched his way through a thicket of bushes toward the campfire ahead. The bright orange flames cut through the darkness. Anxiously he brushed some of the thick branches aside, trying to glimpse the uniforms of the men sitting around the burning wood. He strained to distinguish words among the unfamiliar tones and voices that reached his ears. Suddenly he realized. Only a growth of brushes lay between him and ... a band of Indians!

Haddad shivered, picturing what might occur should he be discovered by Indians on the warpath. He turned quickly and began edging away from the campsite when suddenly an Indian stepped forward. Haddad had been spotted!

One mile away Haddad's son Rafael awoke with a start. His eyes looked around the covered wagon and came to an abrupt halt upon his father's empty bedroll. He jumped down from the wagon and discovered that the horse, too, was missing! Where had his father disappeared to at this hour of night? Something must be wrong. Rafael's heart pounded as he prayed for his father's safety.

Oh, if only everything had gone according to plan. If only they were still back at home in New York.

* * *

It was in September of 1776 in New York. All the grownups had appeared tense for several weeks. Even Rafael's father, who always found time to share a joke or to give him an affectionate slap on the back and inquire about his schoolwork, lately seemed preoccupied. He had time only for the endless meetings that occurred more and more frequently in the synagogue. The cobbled road where Rafael lived seemed changed too. People hurried; children played in houses, not outside. Rafael caught his breath in excitement; there was going to be a war! The colonies would fight to win their freedom from England.

The *Chazan* (leader) of the synagogue strongly urged his followers to ready themselves to move out of the city because it was felt that the British would persecute the Jews. His fears were proven correct when it was later learned that soon after the English did enter New York, they ransacked the synagogue and fired two bullets into a *Sefer Torah* that had been left behind.

Although Rafael had a lively interest in guns and soldiers, his thoughts revolved around something more personal — his approaching *bar mitzvah!* Rafael had been eagerly studying the Torah reading. He was determined to stand before the congregation on the *Shabbos* of his *bar mitzvah* and read the Torah without a single mistake. His parents would be so proud!

He was also studying a *d'var Torah* (speech on a Torah subject). When Meir, his younger brother, got tired of listening to Rafael practice, he enlisted his little sister. Basya would stare up at him as he spoke dramatically and gestured impressively. She was thrilled at this sudden and unusual onslaught of brotherly attention.

Rafael's *bar mitzvah* was only days away. His family was excitedly busy with happy preparations. Mrs. Haddad was joined by members of the congregation in cooking and baking for the big day.

The shadow of war was cast aside as fellow synagogue members came knocking on the Haddads' door, carrying trays of mouth-watering delights. It was the happy custom of their Jewish community to share in the pride and preparation for each family's *simchah*.

Six days before the *bar mitzvah,* Rafael's father came home from a hastily called synagogue meeting with somber news. English troops were arriving in full force at the harbor. The Haddads and a group of other Jewish families must form a wagon train and set out for Philadelphia that very night! As always, Mrs. Haddad was a pillar of strength and she quickly and efficiently organized all the preparations.

Amid the frenzied bustle of activity that followed, Mr. Haddad noticed how slowly and mechanically Rafael was packing. He was sad because he realized that all the *bar mitzvah* plans were canceled. His father saw the look of intense disappointment in Rafael's eyes and led him aside.

He explained that they would make the *bar mitzvah* in Philadelphia. If they remained in New York, Rafael might not be able to have any *bar mitzvah* at all, but with the help of *Hashem,* they would surely complete the long trip before *Shabbos.*

Their conversation was interrupted by the entrance of two men, each carrying a *Sefer Torah* (Torah scroll). The *Sifrei Torah* would be traveling aboard his family's wagon. Rafael bent down, kissing and caressing the soft velvet covers. This precious cargo radiated protection and sudden hope.

He soon found himself bumping along in the wagon, wedged between a chest of drawers and a box labeled "*Pesach dinnerware.*" His newly sewn *bar mitzvah* suit lay carefully folded in a rectangular box, secure on his lap. Clutched in his hand was a bag containing the *tefillin* that were once his grandfather's and were now his. Rafael turned to wave a final goodbye to his old home.

Rafael stared at the shady woods and soft green hills that passed beside the slowly rolling wagon train and a shiver engulfed him. He had overheard his parents discussing in hushed tones the rumor that the English were paying Indians to fight on their side. Late at night it took Rafael a long time to fall asleep. He was frightened. It wasn't pleasant to imagine Indians darting out and attacking them. At this point, Rafael awakened and discovered his father's disappearance.

He waited restlessly. His father had been gone for over two hours. Where was he? Had something happened to him? Would they ever arrive in Philadelphia?

A muffled whimper intruded upon Rafael's racing thoughts. He turned in the direction of the cry and motioned Meir over to his side. He settled his brother close to him on the wagon steps and patted his trembling shoulders. Meir sobbed out how frightened he had been, awakening and noticing his father's empty bedroll. Meir looked up, searching his older brother's face for reassurance. Rafael groped for the words that would comfort his brother and it suddenly didn't matter whether they made it to Philadelphia by *Shabbos*. If only his father would be with him and his whole family could be together, he'd be content wherever his *bar mitzvah* would be.

He thought back to the nights at home when he had lain awake in bed, thinking about how wonderful his *bar mitzvah* would be. He was standing before the *bimah* (Torah-reading table) and captivating the congregation with a magnificent delivery of his *d'var Torah* ... He could smell the grand *Kiddush* prepared in his honor ... He was the center of attention.

Why, all he had been thinking about was his own glory — he never even thought of the true meaning of the *bar mitzvah!* Looking down at Meir's tear-streaked face, Rafael began to think. Becoming a *bar mitzvah* meant grasping opportunities to do *mitzvos,* and assuming responsibilities — such as comforting Meir right now. He hugged his younger brother closer. And it meant facing up to hardships and being a good sport when plans don't work out.

There was well over a *minyan* of men on the wagon train. With his family beside him and the Torah before him he was prepared to become a man right here on the road! Only one thing really mattered:

"*Hashem,* let Father return safely — wherever he is."

Where had he gone?

Rafael didn't know that his father and several other men had unhitched the horses from their wagons and ridden off. They had realized that the caravan had taken a wrong turn and was lost. Leaving most of the men to guard the wagon train, they set off to find the right way to Philadelphia. They separated into groups of three and tried to find assistance. Haddad spotted the campfire in the distance and slowly approached it. Then, before he had a chance to signal his two companions, he was spotted and dragged before the campfire.

He now gazed woefully at the men who lay sprawled around the encampment. Then he gasped. He recognized one of the Indians! His memory went back ten years to the days when he set up his trading post. Indians would often sail down the Hudson River and exchange their furs for his fine European wares. He remembered one in particular.

This young Indian, Red Deer, appeared one day in mid-January. After a lively bartering session Red Deer turned to leave and discovered a heavy blizzard raging outdoors. Realizing that Red Deer was snowbound, Haddad invited him home. Over a hot meal, seated near a friendly fire, the two young men became better acquainted. Several days later Haddad discovered a pile of soft fur heaped upon his front porch. It was an expression of gratitude from his new friend.

Now, he prayed to *Hashem* that the Indian's memory was as good as his.

"Red Deer, don't you remember me?"

The Indian jumped, stared a moment, then ran to Haddad. Red Deer grasped him warmly by his shoulders, while Haddad's fears melted away.

Haddad returned to the wagon train shortly afterward. Red Deer knew the roads and had graciously offered to accompany them part of the way to Philadelphia. He even knew several short cuts that would hasten their arrival.

About to jump onto the wagon, Haddad nearly stumbled over his two young sons who lay fast asleep on the wagon step. Beneath the light of the moon he noticed an expression on Rafael's face that had never been there before. He looked older — as if he were no longer a child; as if he had become ready to accept his true role as a *bar mitzvah.*

Quick Thinking

A story from the Midrash

retold by Rabbi Elchonon (Charles) Wengrov

We all know that it's a sacred duty to study and know the Torah, but we often forget that sometimes it's also very useful — as it was in this case, when the Jews were living in olden Israel.

In a small cottage on the outskirts of Jerusalem, a father and son are talking by candlelight.

"Father, where are you going to this time?"

"To Syria, Shimon. Why do you ask?"

"How I wish I could go with you. It must be wonderful to sail across the sea, and visit strange lands."

"Wonderful? Hardly, my boy. Traveling from the Holy Land to Syria is dangerous. Almost all the sailors on the ships are pirates and cutthroats. You never know if you'll reach port alive. Still ..." and here his father smiled at him thoughtfully. "Are you *sure* you'd like to come with me?"

"Would I!" Shimon's face almost shone with happiness.

"All right," said Zevulun the merchant. "Pack your things in the morning, and take along a *sefer*. You'll have plenty of time to study Torah on the way. I hope your mother won't mind your going, too much."

Young Shimon could hardly sleep that night. At last he was to go with his father on one of those trips to foreign lands. He wondered what Syria was like, and what kind of people lived there. As he dropped off to sleep, he thought about the danger that his father had mentioned. Were the sailors really pirates? At last he fell asleep.

Shimon's mother helped him pack his clothes for the trip. When his bundle was ready, he carried it outside the door of the cottage. Then he ran into his father's room. "I'm all ready, Father," he shouted gaily.

"I told you to wait outside for me." There was a stern look on his father's face. "Why did you come in here?" Shimon just stared, eyes wide open. Inside a bag of clothing his father was packing pieces of gold. Shimon had never seen so much money in his life.

"I'm sorry, Father," he murmured.

"Well, the damage is done. Now you know. Come in. Don't stand in the doorway." Shimon entered slowly, half fearfully. "Now listen to me," said his father. "This money I must take along to pay for the merchandise that I'll buy in Syria. But no one except the two of us must ever know about it until we reach Syria. If anyone else should ever guess that I have this small fortune with me, our lives are in danger. No matter what happens, you are not to say a word, or do anything, to show that you know about it. Not a word or a sign of any kind. Do you understand?"

* * *

The ship was a beauty, made of solid red-brown beams from the cedars of Lebanon and majestic white sails of the sturdiest canvas. It swayed to and fro gently in the blue water. As father and son came aboard, each carrying his bundle of belongings, sailors came forward to help them. Willing hands took up their two bundles, and all walked along the deck to the cabin that was to be their home for the trip.

Suddenly the sailor carrying Zevulun's bundle tripped and fell. Shimon's father's bag slid along the floor, and crashed against the ship's railing. Young Shimon's heart stood still! He wanted to shout, "Be careful! There's money in there!" But his father's stern warning came back to him. He shut his mouth tightly. The bundle was picked up, and they reached the cabin in silence.

Soon the ship began moving. Shimon stood on deck and watched in fascination as the sailors, their solid muscles rippling in the sunlight, hoisted up the large billowing sails, to the tune of a sea chanty. For the next few days he watched whatever the sailors did, enchanted by the strange sights and sounds.

One night, after father and son had finished their simple supper (they had taken along their own kosher food), Shimon was studying quietly from the *sefer* that he had taken along. The small oil lamp flickered slightly, making the black shadows move fitfully on the walls of the cabin. Suddenly, his father put a hand on his shoulder. "Be still a moment," he whispered. There was no sound in the room except the lapping of the water against the ship's hull. Then, from somewhere on deck came the voices of two men talking.

"I say, Demetrios," one voice spoke. "Do you remember what happened the day those two passengers came on board? Remember how I was carrying the old man's bundle?"

"That's right," said the other, "and you tripped and fell."

"Well, when the bundle of his slipped against the railing, I heard something. Do you know what? The clink of gold coins. I know him. He's a rich merchant. He must have a small fortune in that bundle. What do you say? Tomorrow night we can kill the two of them, and drop them overboard. We'll be rich, eh?" There was a grunt of assent.

In the small cabin, Shimon looked at his father, and knew that his father was afraid. For a full five minutes neither of them said anything. Then his father put his hand on Shimon's shoulder.

"All right, my son. Don't fear. *Hashem* is in Heaven, and He won't desert us … Continue studying. What are you studying now, anyway?" Shimon pointed. It was *Koheles* by King Solomon, the beginning of the third chapter. His father looked down, and read: לַכֹּל זְמָן וְעֵת לְכָל חֵפֶץ תַּחַת הַשָּׁמַיִם; עֵת לָלֶדֶת וְעֵת לָמוּת — "For everything there is a season, and a time for every purpose under the heaven: A time to be born, and a time to die …" Then his father's eye fell upon the sixth sentence and he read aloud, half to himself: עֵת … עֵת לְבַקֵּשׁ וְעֵת לְאַבֵּד עֵת לִשְׁמוֹר וְעֵת לְהַשְׁלִיךְ — "A time to seek and a time to lose … a time to keep, and a time to throw away." Zevulun the merchant paced the cabin floor. Then he stopped and turned to his son with a smile on his face. "All right, Shimon. Listen carefully to me…"

* * *

It was noon the next day. All the sailors sat on deck, eating their food. Suddenly they looked up, as Zevulun the merchant came dragging his boy by the hand. The boy was screaming and shouting. In the middle of the deck they stopped.

"So!" Zevulun shouted. "You don't want to go to school in Syria, eh?"

"No! No! I don't want to! Never!"

"After all the trouble I took to get the school to accept you. The finest school in all the world. By heaven, I'll show you. You won't go, eh? Wait here." And Zevulun the merchant ran back to his cabin, seized his bundle of clothing, and returned to his crying, screaming son.

"Do you see this bundle?" shouted Zevulun. "In here I have ten thousand gold pieces, to pay for your expenses in Syria.

Watch!" Before the eyes of an astonished crew he hurled the bundle far out to sea. It sank rapidly. "I'll teach you," Zevulun continued. "You'll live with your uncle, and you'll *work* for a living." And he dragged his son off, back to the cabin.

The voyage came to an end. Once in Syria, father and son rushed from the boat, with only one bundle of clothing. They went to the nearest courthouse, and asked to see the chief judge. Zevulun spoke to him for quite a while, telling about their trip, and how he had been forced to throw his money overboard to save their lives.

It was not long before the sailor who had plotted the murder was arrested, together with his friend Demetrios. The judge spoke harshly to the two sailors:

"Did you plot to kill these two people, and to steal this man's money? I warn you. You were overheard, and if you lie you will be punished."

"It is true, sir," the sailor admitted. "We did plot to kill the two. But what of it? Surely Your Honor can't punish us for what we *wanted* to do. If you put into prison everyone who *wanted* to commit a crime, you would never stop building prisons!"

"That is enough," snapped the judge. "This is my verdict! Because of you this man had to lose ten thousand gold pieces, to save his life. You will pay ten thousand gold pieces, or go to prison."

Within a day the sailor paid the full amount (he had some hidden loot from earlier robberies). As Zevulun the merchant was leaving with his son Shimon, the money in his hand, the judge called out: "Pardon me, Zevulun. If I might ask, how did you ever get such a clever idea — to throw the money overboard in front of the crew?"

"Oh," said Zevulun, "in the Bible there is a sentence that reads: *There is a time to keep, and a time to throw away.* My son was studying it just when we had overheard the sailors." And Shimon blushed.

Moshe's Secret

by Basya Lenchevsky

"**I** never dreamed anything like this camp could ever exist," exclaimed Eliyahu, from Argentina.

"When I was asked to come I was sure it was only a joke. Whoever heard of a camp where boys from all over the world come together?" Simchah, the Israeli, asked.

"I even composed a little poem about it," Ari, the American, said.

"Let's hear it," the other boys pleaded.

"OK., but you better not laugh." With this warning he recited:

> Thirteen tents on grassy knolls,
> An international harvest
> Of one hundred minds and souls.
> Just like young birds still in their nest,
> Needing guidance to be on their own.
> But soon the nest will be empty,
> Off on their own they will have flown.

"That's really beautiful, and it's all true, too. Even the part about going home soon," they sighed.

"I even like the name of this place," another boy piped up, "Camp *Arba Kanfos Ha'aretz* (Four Corners of the Earth). We really are here from all four corners of the world!"

* * *

It was the dream of many people to bring one hundred boys from all over the world together for three short summer weeks. A beautiful spot was found in the country. They decided to use tents to create a rugged type of atmosphere. They wanted the boys to observe nature, the work of *Hashem,* first hand.

Every minute of every day was planned out — learning groups, workshops, *Mussar* (ethics) sessions, swimming and sports. The idea was to get different boys from different backgrounds together and help them understand one another better. Even though their homes were scattered all over the world, they still had one thing in common — the Torah.

The first two weeks were a smashing success. Everything ran smoothly, just as planned. But disaster was already on its way.

The day had started out beautifully, but before nightfall the clouds started gathering. Late at night when everyone was sleeping, thunder crashed and rain fell by the bucketful. A real country thunderstorm! The tents could not stand up to it even though it didn't last long. One by one they collapsed.

When the storm was finally spent, almost one hundred boys crawled out from under their collapsed tents. Much to their surprise they found one tent still standing.

"How did you do it?"

"Is there something different about your tent?"

"Come on, tell us your secret."

Questions flew from all sides at the boys from the lone upright tent.

"We can't understand it either," most of the boys answered. But there was one boy who finally spoke up. "Moshe knows,

make him tell you." With these words he pushed forward a thin Russian boy.

"Tell us, tell us," everyone was jumping up and down with uncontrollable curiosity.

One of the counselors went up to Moshe and asked him quietly if he would like to tell everyone.

"If everyone is interested I'll be glad to tell them, but I think we should fix the tents first and get some sleep. In the morning

I'll be glad to tell you," Moshe answered.

Reluctantly and only after much persuasion, the boys got to work. But the mysterious secret of Moshe's tent was not forgotten. Everyone kept coming up with wild theories, but Moshe kept shaking his head, "No, I'll tell you tomorrow."

* * *

The day dawned bright and sunny with very few traces of the nighttime storm. As soon as *Shacharis* was over Moshe was called upon to tell his story.

"I don't usually like to speak in public but this is an exception," he began. "Since we have come together from many different countries to learn how people can serve *Hashem* all over the world, I feel that my story is very important to you.

"I come from Russia. I am in the United States only a short while. Most of you are homesick for your homelands and will soon be going back. I have no desire to go back to Russia and probably never will. There the government is doing its best to stamp out our religion. So most of us do not know much about Judaism.

"But I was a little luckier than most. My grandfather lived with us the last few years of his life. He was one man who would never give up his religion no matter what anyone did to him. We even had a secret *minyan* (prayer group of ten) in our house and much to everyone's surprise it was never discovered! One by one other *minyanim* were stopped, but never ours. I started bothering my grandfather, 'Zaide, how come they never bother us about our *minyan*?'

"At first he wouldn't answer me but I wouldn't stop asking

him. He finally took me into the room where we prayed. 'Do you see anything unusual here?' he asked me. 'Look by the door.'

"I looked and looked and then I saw it — a rectangular box hanging on the right side of the door frame."

"Oh, you mean a *mezuzah!*" most of the boys shouted.

"Yes, it was a *mezuzah,*" the Russian boy nodded, "but I didn't know what it was then."

Then one boy screamed out, "There's a *mezuzah* hanging on your tent. That must be what saved it."

"You're getting ahead of the story but you're right. Let me just tell you some more about it. This is no ordinary *mezuzah*.

"My grandfather explained to me that a *mezuzah* protects us. We were commanded in the Torah to hang one on every door frame in our house. But since we were living in Soviet Russia there were no scribes to write *mezuzos* and, of course, we weren't permitted to hang them up anyway.

"My grandfather had a desperate visitor one day. He asked to be hidden. The police were following him. Of course Grandfather let him stay. He didn't even ask him what he had done. He was a Jew in trouble. Grandfather did his best to hide him but the man had a feeling that he would be found.

"One day when he seemed especially nervous he handed my grandfather this *mezuzah*. His story came pouring out. He had once been a scribe but the Soviets had found out and forced him to stop writing. Then he decided to start writing again. He knew that *mezuzos* give protection. 'Let Jews just put one up in a back room where nobody would see it,' he would say.

"He had some ink and parchment hidden away, and he

started his secret writing. But somebody told the police. They warned him to stop, but he wouldn't. He escaped just in time. The police were now looking for him.

"Tears streaming down his face, he told my grandfather,

'Please, take this *mezuzah* and hang it up. I am going to leave you now. There's no need for you to get into trouble too.' He left and no word was heard from him. But his *mezuzah* protected us. That is why our *minyan* was never discovered.

"My grandfather left the *mezuzah* to me. It is no ordinary *mezuzah* because it was written with so much *mesiras nefesh* (self sacrifice).

"I knew that we didn't really need *mezuzos* on our tents because they don't have doorposts (and even if they did, we do not need *mezuzos* for a temporary home where we will live for less than thirty days), but I am very attached to my grandfather's *mezuzah* so I brought it along anyway. And now you all see how this *mezuzah* has offered its protection again."

As Moshe concluded his story and the applause died down, Shmuel the head counselor spoke. "We all know that this is no ordinary summer camp. We are here from the four corners of the world. So much planning went into these three weeks, but never in our wildest dreams did we plan or hope for anything like this.

"It was no ordinary story that Moshe told us. Every other tent fell but not the one with the *mezuzah*.

"In fact, every *mitzvah* we have protects us and we have to be sure to do each one correctly. This rule applies all year, but during summertime we must be more careful than usual. We have more free time in the summer; therefore we also have more time to do wrong.

"Let us learn from our friend Moshe, who did more than he had to. *Hashem* rewarded him with extra protection."

Home for Good

by Batsheva Grama

As he did every weekday morning on his way home from *shul,* Menachem Israelson stopped off at the corner *makolet* (grocery store) to pick up fresh bread, milk, and other odds and ends for breakfast and lunch. It was 7 A.M., but that wasn't an unusual time to go shopping in Jerusalem, a city of early risers. The *makolet* was usually busy when Menachem arrived, but he had never seen it as crowded as this! He couldn't even squeeze inside until a few customers pushed their way out with full shopping bags. Once he got inside, he could tell that there was something besides the crowding that was unusual. The atmosphere! On a normal day people were hurried, but friendly and pleasant as they picked up their breakfast necessities before rushing off to school or work. Today, people were impatient and on edge. They argued with the grocer and with each other when he told them he couldn't give them as much as they wanted. Why, Menachem wondered, would that lady need three breads today when she usually took one? And why was that man insisting that he had to have five *kilos* (eleven pounds) of sugar even though the grocer said he was short? People were getting panicky — as if their lives depended on getting every last morsel of food.

The truth was that they really thought their lives depended

on it. The news was bad those days, even frightening. It was May, 1967. President Nassar of Egypt had moved his troops right up to the Israeli border and he was threatening to push the Jews into the Mediterranean Sea. Jews hadn't heard talk like that since the days of Hitler. The U.N., the United States, the Soviet Union, Western Europe — no one was doing anything to prevent an Egyptian invasion. The tension between Jews and Egyptians was so great that it looked as though war would break out any day. That morning the news was even worse. And, like many people when they expect the worst to happen, the people in the *makolet* were trying to stock up on food. Menachem didn't know it, but the same thing was happening in every *makolet* in the country, as frightened mothers tried to make sure they would have enough food for their families in case war broke out.

It had happened before in Israel, but Menachem had never seen it because he was not an Israeli. He and his family had moved from the United States to Jerusalem less than a year ago after his *bar mitzvah* and elementary school graduation. He loved it here — felt as though it was the only real home for him.

The pushing and struggling in the *makolet* was too much for Menachem. He wasn't used to it, he didn't like it, and he refused to do it. He left the *makolet* empty handed and in disgust, but that was nothing compared to the shock that awaited him when he got home.

"Menachem," Mr. Israelson said, trying to look calm and matter-of-fact, but unable to fool his son who could tell that his father was nervous and upset. "You know what's going on at the Egyptian border. It looks very serious. *Imma* and I have been giving it a lot of thought and we came to a decision we wish we didn't have to make. The family is going back to America for a while. We hope it won't be long and as soon as the danger is over we'll be back. Our flight leaves on Sunday morning ..."

Menachem gasped. Without a word he slipped out of the room, ran out to a nearby park, slumped onto a bench, and thought hard. "It won't be for long," his father had said ... but who knew what would happen in the next few months, weeks, or even days? Who knew how long it might take them to return — *if* they returned at all? Sure, life was terrifying in Israel, with people stocking up on food, gloomily preparing bomb shelters, and with the endless army trucks rounding up all available men; but the thought of leaving his beloved *Eretz Yisrael* terrified him even more.

Menachem himself could never pinpoint exactly why he loved living in *Eretz Yisrael* so much. But then again, *kedushah* (holiness) is something that one can't exactly pinpoint either. Somehow Menachem felt that *Hashem* was much closer to him here. He noticed that his Torah learning, as well as his observance of *mitzvos,* had greatly improved since he arrived in the Holy Land. Though he couldn't actually be at the *Kosel* and some of the other sacred places because they were in Jordanian hands, it thrilled him just to know they were so near. He loved living among the religious people here; the beautiful simplicity of their daily lives, the sincerity with which they served *Hashem,* the way they celebrated each holiday together — all this Menachem couldn't live without.

"No, no! I *can't* leave *Eretz Yisrael!* Somehow I must

convince *Abba* and *Imma* to let me stay ..."

It wasn't easy. But, after much discussion, he succeeded. That Sunday the Israelsons' dreaded moment of departure finally arrived — dreaded because they, too, hated to leave *Eretz Yisrael,* and dreaded because they were leaving behind their oldest son in a country whose future looked bleak.

Unfortunately, the Israelsons' timing was perfect — the very next day the ugly war finally broke out. As much as everyone saw it coming, when it actually arrived, people were taken by surprise, and Menachem was one of them. That morning he had decided to *daven* in the Mirrer *Yeshivah,* since it was near his uncle's home where he was staying. After *davening,* just as he was about to leave, a sudden, not-too-distant, thunderous *"BOOM!"* warned him to stay in the building. It was the noise of an exploding bomb and it was soon followed by several more. No one had to announce that the war had begun; and Menachem calmly followed the students downstairs to the dining room and kitchen, which, with the windows covered by sand bags piled high outside, served as the *yeshivah's* shelter. Then, like faithful soldiers, everyone present sprang into action — fighting the enemy by fervently praying and saying *Tehillim* (Psalms). And they were in the war zone; the *yeshivah* was only a few hundred yards from the part of Jerusalem occupied by Jordan.

Menachem had never experienced war before and it was a strange, frightening experience for him. He wondered how he would feel if he were somewhere else in *Eretz Yisrael* at this time. Not as calm, he was sure. Here there was no panic, no hysteria.

These people knew that the soldiers at the front could succeed only with the help of *Hashem* — and the one hundred and fifty people in that makeshift shelter used the weapon of prayer to call for *Hashem's* help. The roar of artillery shells and gunfire kept anyone from forgetting that the danger was constant.

Nightfall. Why do bad things seem to get worse when darkness falls? The non-stop Torah study and prayer was

temporarily halted as the *yeshivah* cooks served supper for the students and trapped guests. Mealtime gave people a short rest from the intensity of the prayers and the tension of the day.

"Israelson," called a neighbor of Menachem, "what are you doing here? You are supposed to be in America."

"My family went, but I wanted to stay."

"I can't understand how your parents let you stay, and I think you're crazy for staying. Don't you hear the explosions? We'll be lucky to get out of here alive."

Menachem was shocked at these words. He remembered a time a few months before when he was taking a walk with his father and they passed the barbed wire fence that divided Jerusalem in two. Looking across the border they could see Jordanian soldiers holding submachine guns. Every once in a while someone accidentally went too close to the border and was shot at, sometimes hit or even killed. Mr. Israelson explained to Menachem how danger, constant danger, could change people, how it could make them frightened and irritable — or brave and understanding.

Menachem thought about what his father said as he wondered what to say to the person whose fear made him say such a terrible thing. Menachem looked around the table and saw people looking angrily at the one who said it. They were on the side of the American youngster.

Before anyone could answer there was an enormous roar and the whole building shook — the *yeshivah* had been hit!

"Fellow Jews! Back to the *Tehillim*," someone called out and in seconds the prayers began again while half full plates remained on the table. Minutes later, there was another crash and again the building shook. Another hit. The prayers grew louder as pieces of plaster fell from the basement ceiling.

Only once during that terrible night did a little voice inside Menachem meekly suggest, "Maybe you should have left with *Abba* and *Imma* ..." but it was quickly silenced as Menachem realized that "danger" and "safety" are very flimsy terms; *Hashem* can change danger into safety in a split second — and the most confident, secure people can find themselves face to face with death. The only safety is faith in *Hashem,* and Menachem knew that his staying in *Eretz Yisrael* helped him get a better hold on that faith.

What an impact the third shell had as it destroyed part of the *yeshivah's* roof! It made the building tremble worse than the two previous hits. And the people inside continued on, wondering if they might be buried in the rubble of another hit or two.

The next hit never came. As morning finally arrived, so did a soldier who informed the brave group that the danger in their area was finally over, and everyone could come out. Later they found out that a huge shell had hit the roof — but had not exploded! If it had blown up, the whole building might have collapsed. No, there was no great sigh of relief, nor celebration; the people all knew that even though they as individuals might be safe, other Jews were still in danger. The prayers and special all night sessions of Torah study continued in all *yeshivos* and most synagogues until the war ended.

They had only five more days to wait, for *Hashem* had mercy on us and made the war end miraculously fast. But that's not the

happy ending of our story. That came a few weeks later when Menachem's uncle said he was going up north to visit relatives and asked Menachem to come along. To his surprise, their car drove into the airport and then Menachem understood. His family was coming back — back *home* again for good.